WILLIA

VIOLIN MAKERS
since
—1702—

MAPLE and PINEWOOD

AFFORDABLE
*and*
LUXURY MODELS

BESTand CHEAPEST
HOUSE
IN THE KINGDOM

TRY OUR INSTRUMENTS AT OUR SHOP IN
36, DARTMOUTH STREET, LONDON

*rothers.*

— USE —
PRIDE OF THE KITCHEN
SOAP.
For Scouring Tin and Woodenware.    For Sale by
BLOOMINGDALE BROS.

WALLACE & RENFURM

ON STAGE FOR

ROYAL OPERA HOUSE
SINCE
—1787—

MALLORY GOLD
COCOA

MALLORY
GOLD
COCOA
TRADEMARK

BEST
*of*
SWEETNESS

From the Pages of the Renowned Rewiew All the Year Round

THE MOONSTONE

A MASTERLY ROMANCE BY
WILKIE COLLINS

Now in book form - in large type and finely illustrated -
published by TINSLEY BROTHERS - 18, Catherine Street - Strand - LONDON

Sherlock, Lupin & Me is published by Capstone Young Readers
A Capstone Imprint
1710 Roe Crest Drive
North Mankato, Minnesota 56003
www.capstoneyoungreaders.com

Text by Pierdomenico Baccalario and Alessandro Gatti
Editorial project by Atlantyca Dreamfarm S.r.l., Italy
Translated by Chiara Pernigotti

Original edition published by Edizioni Piemme S.p.A., Italy
Original title: Ultimo atto al teatro dell'Opera

International Rights © Atlantyca S.p.A., via Leopardi 8 - 20123 Milano – Italia -
foreignrights@atlantyca.it- www.atlantyca.com

Cataloging-in-Publication Data is available at the Library of Congress website.

ISBN: 978-1-4342-6522-7 (library binding)
ISBN: 978-1-4342-6525-8 (paperback)
ISBN: 978-1-62370-158-1 (paper-over-board)
ISBN: 978-1-62370-242-7 (ebook)
ISBN: 978-1-4965-0081-6 (ebook)

**Summary:** Irene Adler, Sherlock Holmes, and Arsène Lupin plan to reunite in London, but
Lupin doesn't show up . . . his father, Théophraste, has been arrested for murder!

**Designer:** Veronica Scott

Printed in China by Nordica.
0414/CA21400605
032014    008120NORDF14

IRENE ADLER

# SHERLOCK, LUPIN & ME

# THE SOPRANO'S LAST SONG

by Irene Adler
Illustrations by Jacopo Bruno

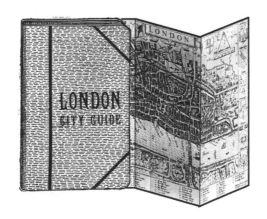

capstone
young readers

# TABLE OF CONTENTS

# Chapter 1

# RESTLESS DAYS, RESTLESS NIGHTS

It is difficult for me to admit — even many years after the Franco-Prussian War — that in those horrible days when the Prussian army was attacking Paris, I could think only about the two wonderful friends I had said goodbye to at the end of the summer — Sherlock Holmes and Arsène Lupin.

Those days, the French Army was in retreat after their shameful defeat at the Battle of Sedan. The Prussian forces were now closing in on Paris, and they showed no signs of stopping.

Luckily, Sherlock was safe, far away from France,

while Lupin, wherever he was, was someone who could take care of himself. So I cannot say I was worried for their safety.

Back then, my thoughts were far more foolish and my youthful heart was beating fast.

All of Paris was talking about our good country's defeat, our sudden fall under Prince Albert of Saxony's bayonets. Some people argued that a truce with the Prussians was necessary to restore the peace. Many people, however, kept up the resistance, joining patriot groups and fighting to defend every corner of the city, ready to die for the cause.

In the meantime, I, Irene Adler, rode in a carriage among the frightened crowds in the streets. While others were out fighting for what they believed in, I was relaxing in a lovely home in Saint Germain des Près while my foster parents were deciding what to do amidst the war that surrounded us.

Yes, my foster parents. Back then, in my naïveté, I never questioned my origins. I had never considered why my small, freckled face, bright hair, and blue eyes did not resemble that of my mother or father.

Reflecting on it now, I realize there were many things I chose not to think about back then.

There were other things that made me restless when I thought about them. War, of course.

But my most pressing thought was another one. Among all those headlines and announcements, all the homes blackened from fire, and all the soldiers in their imperial uniforms that were torn to pieces, all I could think was . . . *where were Sherlock and Lupin?*

I remember all the support people offered me then: I did not have to worry, nor be scared, they told me. Indeed, many wealthy, young girls were just that — not worried, nor scared. And it was these young girls my mother hoped I might befriend.

Some of these unworried girls and their mothers happened to be in our living room that Tuesday in September 1870 when I begin my story.

When I spotted them arriving at our house from my bedroom window, I thought they looked like ducks marching in a line toward a lake. But instead of shimmering feathers, my mother's friends and their daughters (for these girls were not my friends at all) were showing off fancy blue, pink, and yellow dresses. Their boring eyes were hidden underneath delicate hats with veils, and their pale, soft hands sported smooth khaki gloves. They carried small silk fans and wore all the jewelry a thief could ever hope for.

Bakeries in Paris were already rationing bread, and many shops throughout the city were showing sad, empty shelves. Considering this, I should have been very upset about all that unnecessary frill.

But I often found myself behaving like a child in that house. Back then, I pretended to be quieter and more cooperative with my parents than I really was.

It was only when I was with my two best friends, Sherlock and Lupin, that my spirit was set free. And it was during these moments that my mind uncovered the reckless emotions and thoughts I never before knew I had.

\* \* \*

The Parisian society ladies were in the living room, and I was in my bedroom. Mr. Horatio Nelson, our butler, hovered like an owl outside my door.

"Miss Irene," he called. "Your mother is waiting for you."

He didn't call as much as sigh.

I looked at the two letters that were lying on my desk and sighed back to him. "I'll be there right away," I lied, unable to look away from the willowy, elegant handwriting that covered the longer note — the one Sherlock had given me the day I left Saint-Malo that summer.

I knew what he wrote to me by heart. I had read that note many times on the road back to the city and many times in the days following.

Sherlock wished me all the best for my journey home, and for the first time since we met, he mentioned the violence and chaos that was going on in France. We were far away in Saint-Malo, protected by our distance from the war and by the slowness of the mail service. Because of this, we were able to ignore most of the threats that our home country faced that summer.

But when summer was over, I returned to Paris, while Sherlock went to London with his family.

London . . . from his letter it seemed that Sherlock was convinced everything would be perfect there. And he was starting violin lessons! That news made me smile.

Imagining Sherlock playing the violin . . . it was like picturing Arsène Lupin wearing a priest's robe! Sherlock seemed too anxious and impatient to master an art that required so many boring and repetitive exercises.

I say this with some humor, but . . . the truth?

The truth is that I spent some sleepless nights, surrounded by the white light of the moon, picturing Sherlock Holmes standing by me and playing his violin. While cannons and gunfire rumbled just outside of Paris, was this just my way to avoid thinking about the war that was moving closer to my city?

The rest of Sherlock's letter was hasty. He wrote that he hoped someday I could get to London or he to Paris — maybe when the war was over, when it was not so dangerous to travel. The letter ended this way:

> *Either way, I promise to take you to the most discreditable and disreputable places in town when we are together again!*

> *Yours, Sherlock Holmes*

I had just finished reading it again when Mr. Nelson gently knocked on the door once more and told me I had to go downstairs . . . our company was asking for me. But I did not want to give much of my time to those guests — not more than was necessary.

"Come in, Mr. Nelson," I said, folding the letter from Sherlock.

"I am not the one who needs to come *in,* Miss Irene," Mr. Nelson reminded me, pulling the door open. "You are the one who needs to come *down.* The ladies are waiting for you."

Raising an eyebrow, I asked, "And what do they need from me exactly? My knowledge of Latin poetry, my opinion on fashion during war, or just my unique sense of humor?"

"The last thing you said, Miss." He smiled.

Now I can easily say it: I got along much better with Mr. Nelson than with my mother.

Don't be shocked, please. It was nobody's fault.

For I was not a good girl.

And she was not my mother.

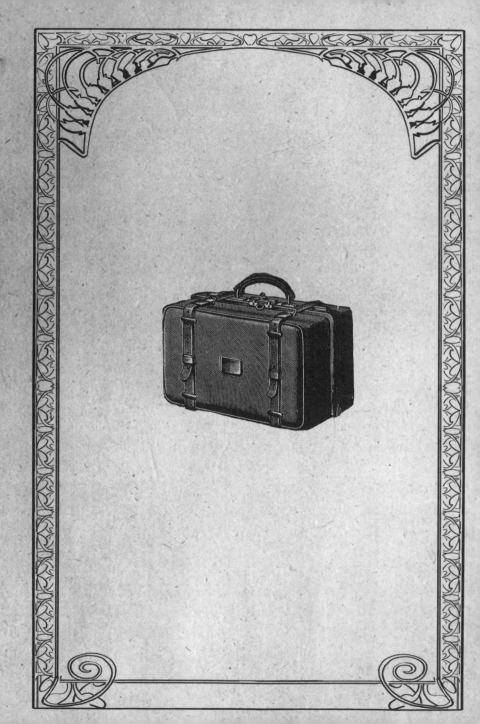

# Chapter 2

# LIKE A LIGHTNING BOLT

"This tea is really delicious!" squeaked the young girl dressed in white. She was perched on a small couch in our living room like a curlicue of cream atop a pastry.

I ignored her — as an act of survival for us both — and gazed out the tall windows of our living room. The very air seemed thin. Big clouds were speeding westward across the sky. They made me think about how time was passing so quickly and how I was wasting it, letting it melt away like sugar in hot tea. I had been with these women and their daughters for less than fifteen minutes, and I already felt overwhelmed with boredom.

I knew that Mr. Nelson was standing just behind one of the living room doors, and I envied him. He, at least, could smile in secret about the useless habits, the unkind gossip, and the meaningless conversations these women had.

My mother seemed to love these things so much. She told me she had missed the company during our vacation in Saint-Malo.

During the months we spent at the coast, her tiny, pale face did not tan even a little bit, and her slow and proper movements seemed to get even slower.

And how did she describe the time she spent on the beautiful Normandy coast to her friends?

*Boring.*

She managed to highlight all the problems she had with a place that I, on the other hand, thought was quite lovely.

*Much better than being in Sedan!* That's what I wanted to say to remind her . . . at the same time we were vacationing on the coast of France, people were dying in battle on the opposite side of our country. But it would have been rude to say that.

I did not want to hurt my mother . . . I simply wanted not to be sitting there with that dull crowd.

So I decided on a sort of compromise. I would throw a small stone, so to speak, into the motionless waters of the conversation.

"This morning I heard some gunshots here in the main square. Have you heard anything?" I asked, biting into a piece of coffee cake. "It sounds like someone probably died!"

"Someone died?"

"Why was he killed?"

"Was he married?"

The little cuckoos got excited.

And once again I wished I could have seen Mr. Nelson's face.

Bored by the chatter, I began to think of my friend Arsène Lupin. He had written to me a couple of days after I left Saint-Malo. It was lucky that his brief note got to me despite the war.

He wrote just a few lines. While it did not have the nice, lengthy sentences that Sherlock's letter had, it was no less interesting. He wrote that he had been thinking about me for days, and I thought that admitting it to himself must have been difficult.

On the back of the postcard he wrote:

*I'm leaving with my father, looking for shows. I hope you're doing well and that we can meet again. Don't try to get back to me — I don't know what address I'll be at. Kisses.*

The way Lupin ended that letter showed all his confusion. *Kisses.*

Like it was normal to write this type of thing to a friend like me. Or like it was normal to kiss me.

The truth?

The truth is that while one of the prissy girls babbled on about some singing teacher at the Academy, I imagined Lupin's face — his high cheekbones and floppy, black hair — right in front of my eyes. And I considered what it would be like to kiss him.

At the very thought, I blushed and laughed out loud, almost pouring tea on my dress.

"Irene? Is everything all right, my dear?" my mother asked. Her eyes were troubled.

My mother was charming. I say this without my usual sass. She could be admirable in a certain way.

She could pretend she was talking to me while she was actually talking to her friends. While she was afraid of my unpredictability, she needed me there to show off what a wealthy and respectable family we were.

We could drink tea and have cookies even while the empire was falling apart!

I did not want to oppose her, even if it was difficult for me. I would rather be in the library with my books, or (I wish!) walking around town with Sherlock and Lupin.

But I was a girl, and from a good family. All the things that might have been allowed to a son were forbidden to me.

"Everything's fine, Mother," I answered.

I held in a yawn for all that surrounded me. It seemed unbelievable to me that while a whole army was marching toward the capital, people could waste away their days in a sitting room.

The torture lasted for another hour, until, thank goodness, my father came home. Slamming the front door behind him, he managed to dodge the staff and barge into the living room with his coat dripping water on the floor.

"Leopold!" my mother immediately scolded him.

The clouds in the sky were thick now. They let loose an angry, noisy rain on the city.

"How lovely!" I exclaimed. "It's raining!"

Our guests gazed at me, shocked, from around the room.

"Irene!" my father greeted me enthusiastically. Then he added right away, "Good afternoon, ladies!"

He looked at me with those sharp eyes that made him look like a mischievous child — not like the railway and iron mogul that he was.

I looked back at him, feeling my cheeks burn under my mother's envious gaze. Every time she saw Papa and me together she seemed to be wondering what the secret was behind the bond we shared.

"Go pack your bags!" my father said. "Both of you, go pack your bags. Next week Ophelia Merridew will be at Covent Garden, where she will be performing in the latest work of the famous Giuseppe Barzini!"

"Ophelia Merridew?" I answered in shock. She was the best opera singer of all time.

"Covent Garden?" my mother asked, nearly jumping out of her chair. Since there was no theater

in Paris by that name, she added: "Covent Garden —
where, my dear?"

"We're going to London!" my father said, excited.

It's not difficult to imagine that my father's
announcement created tension in the quiet Adler
family.

But what I did not know then was that my life
would be changed completely because of that piece
of news . . . and because of the events that followed.

\* \* \*

That evening, dinner was served at 7:30. We had a
hearty chicken soup. I entertained myself by floating
croutons on top and counting how long it took them
to sink, while my parents began discussing London.

They had not talked about it yet, because my
mother thought it was impolite to do so in front of
her guests — even if the ladies, of course, would not
have left anyway. Minding someone else's business
was too much of an attraction for some women!

"So this Ophelia, my dear —" my mother started.

That was all my father needed to begin a
passionate review of the singer's hits, list a summary
of the positive responses she had received from

critics around the world, and an account of how Merridew enchanted every audience for whom she performed.

"But, Leopold, in this circumstance . . ." my mother said. "Circumstance" was the strongest word she ever used to refer to war.

I sipped a spoonful of broth. I guess I was too loud, because they realized I was there.

"Even Irene loves her," my father said. "Don't you, sweetie?"

I nodded. I did not have to pretend. Ophelia Merridew was the role model of almost every singing teacher I'd ever had.

"Mrs. Gambetta says that Ophelia's voice is outstanding, and that having the chance to listen to her is an absolute privilege," I said.

"See, my dear?" my father said. "An absolute privilege. And do you really want to give up an absolute privilege in times like these?"

"Leopold . . ." My mother sighed. "Irene and I only just came back from our vacation at the coast. I'm exhausted. Just the thought of traveling again frightens me. And how would we get there? Is transportation even running? I heard that the whole city is shut down and that there's a mass of people coming to Paris from the countryside —"

My father made his lips snap. "Nonsense," he said. "I have already planned everything."

"You have already planned . . . without asking my opinion?" she asked.

"Oh, come on dear!" he countered.

"Don't be pushy, Leopold."

"I'm not being pushy."

"Yes you are."

They kept arguing in their usual style. It was like witnessing a bizarre fight between knights wearing rubber armor, the sword strikes just bouncing off one another.

Even if I did not have the slightest idea what was really happening in Paris, I understood what Papa was trying to do. He was trying to send us as far away from the war as possible.

During a break in the argument, I intervened, "Mrs. Gambetta said that if only Ophelia had come to Paris, she would have done anything to take us students to see her. Because you cannot know the true essence of song if you haven't heard her sing."

A long, embarrassed silence followed. It was my

mother who pushed me to take singing lessons, for she considered a good singing voice necessary to be part of the high-class society.

"Did she really say that?" Papa asked, satisfied by my support.

The truth was that Mrs. Gambetta was convinced that she herself was better than the most renowned opera singer of that time. She thought that by simple bad luck, no one could appreciate her voice. That, or there was some type of conspiracy against her.

"Yes," I confirmed anyway. "That's exactly what she said."

I avoided looking into my mother's eyes, but I felt shivers down my spine.

"And when did Mrs. Gambetta listen to, uh . . ." she whispered, rattling her silverware, "Ophelia Merridew?"

"Oh," I answered. "You'd have to ask her."

"If Mrs. Gambetta said that, though . . ." my father whispered, taking a big sip of wine.

Mama did not reply. She was defeated. I had to stop myself from glancing at my father.

"So, are we really going?" I asked while Mr. Nelson took the dishes away.

"Well . . ." Papa answered. He wore a big smile. It was a polite way of acknowledging his victory.

I went upstairs to my bedroom just in time to avoid listening to more of their argument. From the stairs, I could still hear bits of their conversation. I went to my desk, grabbed some paper, ink, and an inkstand, sat down, and stared into the shaky light from the oil lamp.

I did not write a single word. I stood up and opened my window, letting the soft noise of the rain into the room.

The city was dark, and a curfew was in place. It was so quiet that each step on the sidewalk roared. I saw lightning far away to the east, and I pictured soldiers falling on the front line, wherever that was now. I could not even imagine it: war.

I thought about London, and, of course, I thought about seeing Sherlock and maybe Lupin again . . . if one of his father's adventures landed him there.

At the bottom of his letter, my English friend had left an address. Maybe, once I got there, I could try to stop by and say hello.

Or maybe it would be better to let him know beforehand that I was coming. What were the odds that a letter sent during war could get there before its sender?

I sat down again, staring at the blank piece of paper. I chewed my pen, and then I began writing.

*My dear Sherlock,*

*You cannot imagine what just happened to me . . .*

★ ★ ★

The next morning, I hurried downstairs looking for Mr. Nelson. I found him standing at the front door, staring at the road that was still wet with rain.

I handed him the envelope holding the letter I had written last night and asked, "What say you, Horatio Nelson? Will it get there in time?"

Mr. Nelson took the envelope and read the name on it. He did not look surprised. He smiled and began walking away, taking the letter to whatever post office was still open in this war-torn city.

"Mr. Nelson?" I called to him.

"What is it, Miss Irene?"

"Will you come to England with us?" I asked.

He answered, raising the envelope as if to suggest a link between the letter and what he was about to say. "Your mother, Miss Irene, has asked me to look after you when she is not there and has told me not to leave you alone for a second."

*Why would she not be there?* I thought. *Does that mean she isn't coming to London with us? And why not?*

I quickly ran inside and found my mother fully dressed, eating breakfast.

When I asked if it was true that she would not be coming with us, she said, "I won't leave my house. I won't leave everything we have to those barbarians."

At that point, I couldn't imagine the looting and destruction that would haunt this town after battle. Could it be, perhaps, that my mother had a better grasp on this matter than I did as a young girl?

"And what did Papa say?" I asked.

"He said that this house is not important," she answered mysteriously.

What he had *actually* said, I would later learn, was that the house and our belongings were not more important than our safety. He told her that if he could not take us all away, he would at least take me away.

# Chapter 3

# THE BLUE TRAIN

Considering it was the end of September, it was unusually cold the morning we left for London. My mother, in an effort to point out how opposed she was to the trip, chose not to even change out of her nightgown. She came to say goodbye and stood at the front door, wrapped up in a long robe with her hair undone.

I, on the other hand, was presentable for once. My hair was brushed, I wore a skirt that my Parisian non-friends would have found cute with my long legs, and I sported a pair of shoes with laces. I stood

SHERLOCK, LUPIN & ME

on my toes to kiss my mother goodbye, and I smelled something bad on her, something that, years later, I would learn was alcohol.

She got close to me — so close that she surprised me, as that was probably the first time I felt the touch of her body.

"You will be careful, right, Irene?" she whispered in my ear.

I remember that moment very well.

The person I saw at the front door that morning was a real person, showing all her stubbornness, fears, and weaknesses. It was as if the mask of etiquette behind which my mother always hid had slipped away.

While we hugged, I wanted to tell her that I had never felt that close to her. But I didn't.

Since then, I've learned that the most important words, the real ones, often get trapped somewhere between heart and mouth and never come out. This is what happened to me in that moment.

"Of course, Mama. You take care yourself," was all I managed.

My mother was not used to being defenseless for too long. I felt her arms get rigid with embarrassment.

And when our eyes met again, she was back to being the distant mother that I knew all too well.

She turned toward Mr. Nelson, who stood at the door, and gave him instructions on a number of things. Then she made sure that all our luggage was in the carriage.

As she did so, Papa came downstairs from his bedroom. He looked at me, smiling, and then said, "Come on, come on! The train won't wait for us!"

He affectionately patted my back as he prodded me down the stairs to the street. I knew that his hurrying me to the carriage was an effort to keep me away so my parents could have a private goodbye. I did as I was told, but I sat by a window in the carriage so I could witness the whole scene without them knowing. Mama and Papa faced one another for a few seconds. She shook her head and said the word "crazy." He gestured around them, as if to say that it was more crazy to stay in Paris.

Then Papa grabbed her hands and pulled them toward him, asking her one last time to come with us. She shook her head, looking upset.

But this wouldn't convince my father to stay. He then shook his head, kissed her forehead, and walked toward Mr. Nelson and me, while Mama slipped down into a chair like a withered flower.

★ ★ ★

Our black carriage crossed deserted roads and crowded squares. Many Parisians were meeting up for protests or rallies. There were men building a barricade with furniture, perhaps to hold off the Prussians.

I grabbed onto the window, asking my father, "Is this dangerous?"

"Yes," he said, quite frankly.

He beat the coachman box with his cane to make the horse go faster.

We arrived at the big train station, Gare du Nord, and the carriage left us right on the platform. Papa grabbed my arm as if he was afraid of losing me, and guided me to our train track. And then the three of us, Papa, Mr. Nelson, and I, got on a blue train headed to Boulogne-sur-Mer.

The train whistled so sharply that I had to cover my ears. A few seconds later, the train began its slow march. A cloud of steam surrounded the train cars and then disappeared in the cold air.

I finally relaxed in my seat. It was like I had just realized what was happening to me . . . I was traveling to London!

My father was already busy with his newspaper, and Mr. Nelson held a book written by the American author Edgar Allan Poe. Mr. Nelson told me he liked Mr. Poe, but thought his writing was too vulgar to be suitable for me.

I fumed. I hated that other people could decide what was suitable for me and what was not. But I was only unhappy for a few minutes.

I got wrapped up in the beauty of the landscape outside my window — an endless green plain, interrupted only by some low hills.

"Just a few years ago," said my father, lowering his paper and gazing at the beautiful French countryside. "Actually, *some* years ago, when I was your age, a trip like this would have taken at least a couple of days. We would've had to change horses twice, stop to eat, sleep, check our packages . . ."

When he said that, I thought about my letter to Sherlock. *Did the letter leave before us, and did my friend know about our arrival?* I wondered.

"And now look . . . progress!"

We quickly stopped in Amiens, where many people got on and off the train. Leaning on the window, I realized that our blue train was full of people and luggage. It seemed that it was just the three of us who had the privilege of having our own compartment.

Three hours later, we arrived at the Boulogne -sur-Mer station.

"And now?" I asked my father.

"Now come with me," he said, cutting me off like I was one of his employees.

I was not offended by it, however. I looked at his eyes, which sparkled with enthusiasm like a child's and could not be angry. We either understood each other in a heartbeat or not at all, my father and I.

Mr. Nelson went to check on the luggage to make sure it followed us to the ferry, but my father was already making his way through the crowd in the station.

"Papa!" I shouted to get his attention. "What about Mr. Nelson?"

Like a soldier who had just been whipped between his shoulder blades, Leopold Adler straightened his back and stopped.

"Oh yes!" he said, emerging from his thoughts. "Where is he?"

Our butler found us a few minutes later. "Luggage is going to the ferry, sir," he said, but Papa wasn't listening. He started to walk again, satisfied that Mr. Nelson was by my side.

"What's wrong with him?" I asked.

Mr. Nelson shrugged. "And with you, Miss Irene?"

I looked at him. *How did he always understand what was on my mind?*

"I'm thinking about London," I answered.

"London?" He smiled. "Or is it someone living in that city?"

"The truth is, I'm thinking about two people. Not just one," I quipped.

"Ah, Miss Irene!" exclaimed Mr. Nelson, half serious. "Such friendships are not suited to a young lady like you! One of these days your mother is going have a fit about it. You know that, right?"

Instead of answering, I asked him a question. "And what would good friendships be like, Mr. Nelson? The daughters of my mother's friends? Goodness no! Can you picture me talking about weddings, shoes, and hats all day long?"

"If you really want to know my opinion, Miss Irene, I actually do not think those things suit you. But maybe you can find some friendships that do not involve murders and criminals."

"Sherlock and Lupin are not criminals!" I exclaimed.

"I didn't say that," Mr. Nelson said kindly. "But I don't think I need to say anything else, do I?"

"What are you suggesting, Mr. Nelson?"

"Nothing more than what I said, Miss Irene. I hope you'll have the chance to meet your friends once again. And I also hope that a meeting doesn't mean a —"

We were interrupted by my father, who stood in the middle of the street ahead of us, cursing.

We reached him in front of the battered door of a dilapidated building.

"I can't believe it! This is the best inn in town!" he complained. The building looked like it had had some bad luck in recent years. "I came here with my father many years ago, when I was a boy, and I can assure you, I have never had such delicious duck breast in my entire life."

His mustache made his expression look even

more disappointed, the ends of it curling around the edges of his frown.

I laughed, and my father stared at me. "It's a disgrace, I'm telling you! A disgrace!" he shouted.

"I wish you could see yourself, Papa!" I said, still laughing.

He opened his eyes wide, but when he saw that even Mr. Nelson could not contain his laughter anymore, he started to laugh with us.

And with a nice, big laugh, we all went to have dinner at another restaurant, Grand Cochon. Instead of duck breast, we enjoyed three wonderful baked pork legs with potatoes.

# Chapter 4

# AN UPSETTING ENCOUNTER

I spent the whole afternoon on the ferry deck with my father. I will always remember the time we spent together, not speaking, watching the bow of the steamboat splitting the waves with such ease.

Mr. Nelson wisely decided to stay inside, for our brave butler was prone to motion sickness.

I enjoyed the breeze in my hair as I breathed in the salty air. I looked out over the bow, hoping to spot England like many other passengers. I knew that only one person could be the first to scream "Land!" and I had bet Papa that I would be that person.

But as we sailed away from the coast, the pleasant breeze became cold, the sky slowly darkened, clouds gathered over the sea, and heavy rain started to fall.

"We should get inside," Papa said. "Otherwise we'll be spending our first days in London in bed." He was right, of course, so I had to give up on my bet.

We sat at a table, where we ordered some hot tea and butter cookies. Mr. Nelson went down to the lowest level in the ferry where he couldn't see the stormy, gray sea. I realized that he left the book by Mr. Edgar Allan Poe on the bench. I grabbed it and started reading right away.

Papa laughed and chatted with some fellow businessmen until the ferry began to slow.

"Here we are!" people started to exclaim. I had to force myself to abandon my book. Wow, that American knew how to write — and his story was scaring me to death!

I leaned on the porthole and gazed out over the water. A ray of light tore through the clouds like a blade, and suddenly I could see the famous White Cliffs of Dover. I was so amazed, I could barely open my mouth.

We were in England, and I had spotted the cliffs before anyone else. But before I could say anything, I heard a lady yell to her husband, "Land! Look, Philippe! No, that way! We're there!"

★ ★ ★

With a huge crowd of people greeting us, my father and I walked down the ramp to the dock. Mr. Nelson was one of the first people off the boat, and once on solid ground, he made the sign of the cross.

As we found Mr. Nelson waiting for us on the dock, I thought, happily, that England seemed much like France so far. The albatrosses flew low, circling over the piles of suitcases on the dock. Down the street, I could see sailors, people on vacation, and carriages moving about. We headed toward the action, looking for a carriage that could take us to the train station.

Distracted by all the noise and yelling at the port, we lost sight of one another in the crowd. While I looked around to find my father and Mr. Nelson, I saw a guard yelling at a homeless person.

As I watched, the homeless person suddenly began running toward me. Someone tried to grab him, but he easily managed to get away. He was onto me in a heartbeat.

I felt him grab my arm and saw a pair of hungry eyes that looked at me as if they could see inside my soul. It felt like I was in one of Mr. Poe's scary stories.

My legs gave out and I fell to the ground. The homeless man then let me go, jumped up, and disappeared into the crowd.

"Irene!" Papa yelled as he hurried forward. He lifted me off the ground as easily as he might lift a bird. "Irene, what happened? Is everything okay?"

"Y-yes," I answered, still in shock.

"Miss Irene!" Mr. Nelson came running.

"Horatio, you fool!" my father scolded. "I told you to always be with her!"

I had never heard him talk that way to Mr. Nelson.

"I'm sorry, Mr. Adler. I . . . got distracted for a second and . . ."

"It's not his fault," I said. "It was just a homeless person running away."

"Nasty thieves!" said my father. "Did he steal anything from you? Is everything with you?"

I touched my pockets and then made sure my purse was intact. "No, he didn't take anything."

"Sure?"

I nodded. Actually, the homeless man had done the opposite of stealing, as I would find out later on. He *gave* me something.

Once we were settled in our seats on the train to London, I reached in my purse to give Mr. Nelson his book back and I found a folded piece of paper in my fingers instead. Not sure what it was, I opened it.

As soon as I laid my eyes on the script, I felt my heart beating fast in my throat. It took me a second to recognize Sherlock Holmes's handwriting.

"Oh!" I said. "Coward!"

So those eyes that stabbed at me were *his?*

I had to breathe deeply to calm myself enough to read what he had written. No greeting, no "My dear Irene" — this letter took a more decisive tone:

*I hope you haven't become too posh since I last saw you and that you weren't expecting a traditional greeting! Anyway, welcome to good old England. By a lucky coincidence, our friend Arsène Lupin is in London with his father now, too. Meet at Shackleton Coffee House, 11 Carnaby Street, on Monday morning, 10 sharp. Lupin and I will be there!*

# Chapter 5

# OPHELIA THE DIVINE

I could not fall asleep that night. The room at the Claridge's Hotel was nice and the bed was as soft as whipped cream, but there were too many things that were upsetting me. I kept seeing, again and again, the dark, deep eyes of the homeless man — or, rather, Sherlock Holmes — in Dover.

Thinking again about what had happened, I felt both angered and amused by what Sherlock had done. The gesture *was* original and brave, I'll give him that.

When I wasn't thinking about Sherlock, some

other faces came to mind. Lupin's, of course, since I had not even hoped I would see him again this soon, and then Ophelia Merridew's face, like I had seen it in the paper. Soon I would admire her face in real life, and enjoy the privilege of listening to her enchanting voice. Then I imagined my mother's face, severe and stubborn like when we said goodbye in Paris.

When I finally saw some light coming in from the curtains, I decided to get up. I went down to the lobby and immediately ran into my father.

"I sent a letter to your mother," he said, kissing my forehead. "Everything is set so she can come here without any risk. You probably wondered why I didn't force her to come with us," he continued as we walked arm in arm toward the breakfast tables. "The truth is, I know your mother quite well. And I know that, from time to time, she needs to have her way. Insisting only makes things worse. This way, she usually comes to her senses in a matter of hours!"

We sat at a table and ordered a big English breakfast of eggs benedict, sausages, and a tasty mixture of rice, cod, and spices. We ate while Papa told me his plan for the day. We would make our way around London in a comfortable carriage until dinner, at which point we would return to the hotel for a light meal.

"It's the only way not to tire ourselves out before tonight. Don't you agree, Irene?" he continued, biting into a slice of bread. "Your body will need to be rested, and your spirit awake. The art of the divine Ophelia Merridew deserves no less than that!"

I nodded, enjoying my father's enthusiasm.

Then came an unusual noise . . . something like the sound of soup boiling. I turned and realized that it was the peculiar laugh of a peculiar character sitting at the table beside us. He was a big man, with a round face and a thick beard, and he wore a bright-blue tailcoat. He was looking at Papa and me.

When our eyes met, he said in shaky English, "The gentleman is right!"

"I'm happy to hear you say that, sir," said my father, lifting his cup of tea in a toast.

The man laughed again, in his most unique way, and introduced himself. He was Sergej Trudoljubov, a Russian baron. He traveled all the way from Saint Petersburg to London to see Miss Merridew's show.

The man and my father began discussing opera. "I don't know if he's the greatest composer of all time, but he is my favorite!" declared my father, when the topic had moved on to Giuseppe Barzini.

"We agree again, my friend!" the baron said. "To think that just a few years back, I was among those who thought that the Maestro was done! I was wrong, wasn't I, my friend?"

"Don't be too hard on yourself, sir," my father answered kindly. "At a certain point it did seem like Barzini's inspiration got weaker. But then —"

"Then he fooled everyone like me who had that thought!" the baron finished for him.

That time, the three of us laughed pretty hard.

"His last two works are great once again — so vigorous!" my father commented.

"Certainly," approved Trudoljubov. "I tell you, that genius is living a second youth, my dear friend!"

The baron then bowed and went back to the big plate of sausages that sat in front of him.

★ ★ ★

After our long carriage outing, we returned to the hotel for a quick dinner of soup and meat, then went to get ready in our rooms. Since that night was a special occasion, I wanted to be dressed accordingly.

I spent a good hour in front of the mirror, preparing every detail of my outfit. I was taming one last lock of hair when I heard someone knocking on my door.

"Irene, it's time to go!" said my father. "The carriage is waiting for us!"

I still remember the radiant look Papa gave me when I opened the door in my periwinkle evening gown. "Irene! You're a sight for sore eyes!" he said, taking my arm and leading me out to our carriage.

Just a few minutes later, we arrived at the Royal Opera House in Covent Garden. Papa and I climbed the entrance stairs, moving through the crowd of people. I felt as if a pair of wings had just sprouted from my shoulders, and my heart was beating fast.

At the top of the staircase, my father met a distinguished-looking man, who had two thick, white tufts of hair on his cheeks. His name was Mr. Jabkins. He was a very rich wood merchant who had offered to host us in his box that night.

The entrance was filled with people from all over Europe. I glanced at the people milling between the big white marble columns. I saw old men in diplomatic uniforms, ladies wearing tons of jewels, cadets and young men from the nobility, businessmen sporting black ties . . . it was clear that being here was a privilege very few people had!

Papa and I had just said hello to Baron Trudoljubov when I noticed that several people were staring at three men nearby. I soon realized that one of those men was Maestro Giuseppe Barzini. The other two, much younger than him, I did not recognize. A lady, perhaps noticing my confusion, whispered in my ear, "The tall man with the black mustache is Alfred Santi, Barzini's assistant! A very talented young man, they say. The blond man is a new discovery of the Maestro. Henri Duvel, a Frenchman!"

I thanked her for the information and paused to look at the two young men. I watched as another man introduced himself to Barzini. The two assistants also moved forward to introduce themselves, but they bowed at the same time and their heads collided.

I quickly covered my mouth to hide my amusement at the scene. The two young men, however, did not laugh at all. Santi spoke angrily to the Frenchman who, his face turning red, argued right back. Barzini had to step in to calm them down, and when he did, they immediately shut up. They continued glaring at each other, however.

Soon Mr. Jabkins found my father and me and led us to his box. It was in an excellent spot. I looked through my binoculars. Below us, lines of people moved like waves in a stormy sea. The musicians in the orchestra pit tuning their instruments reflected the anticipation of the crowd. I gazed at the rows of seats, full like flower boxes in spring.

It was then that I met the eyes of a young lady, on the other side of the theater, who looked toward me. She was a very elegant woman, and her face was delicate and pale. As soon as I saw her it was like a switch suddenly flipped in my mind.

Without knowing why, I found myself thinking about the summer that had just passed. I imagined the town of Saint-Malo and I pictured a carriage moving away from me quickly.

I flinched. I had seen that woman before!

But at that moment, the lights dimmed, and the whole theater went dark. Soon the curtains opened, and I forgot the strange feeling I had just a few moments before when I locked eyes with that woman across the theater.

Ophelia Merridew had taken the stage.

# Chapter 6

# IN THE HEART OF THE CITY

It is pointless for me to try to find the right words to express what I felt that night listening to Ophelia Merridew, but I haven't been so stunned and enchanted by anything since.

The piece performed was *The Plot of Destiny* by Giuseppe Barzini. The tragic love story ended when Miss Merridew morphed into an angel, leaving her lover forever. Looking at Ophelia through my binoculars, I was spellbound by her big eyes. They were full of emotion, and the feelings she expressed seemed as real as anything in this world.

Shocked by the sad story we had just watched unfold on the stage, my father and I were quiet as we exited the theater. I remember the trip back to the hotel well. We spent the whole time in silence, and that peaceful silence was only interrupted by a few long sighs that came from his or my lips.

Years later, when I thought about moments like these, the fact that Leopold Adler was not my biological father (as I would find out later) lost all its importance. We were father and daughter, and we were, in fact, very similar despite everything.

★ ★ ★

*The Plot of Destiny* left a mark on my soul. That night, I dreamed of Ophelia Merridew. She was wearing a white, angelic gown, and she walked toward me, crossing through a foggy field. I saw a dark look in her eyes. Then she got closer to me and whispered, "Help me!"

I moved closer to hug her, but she was just a shadow. I ran toward her, but I got lost in the fog surrounding me. Then the dream ended and I fell into a deep sleep, which lasted quite a while — too long, to tell the truth.

When I opened my eyes again and turned toward the window, I realized it was late morning. That was one of the strangest sleeps of my life. It was like I had been trapped in a bubble, surrounded by Barzini's music and the voice of the great soprano singer.

But now I was back in the real world, where time passed in its usual way. It was Monday morning already.

"Sherlock! Lupin!" I jumped up from my bed. I ran to open the curtains and glanced quickly at the clock. It was 9:30! I was supposed to be at Carnaby Street in half an hour to meet my friends.

The thought that they might tease me, saying I was "posh" for making people wait, made me hurry to get ready. I was dressed in just a few minutes. I ran downstairs to look for my father in the restaurant, but he wasn't there.

Anxious, I started wandering around the hotel like a fool. I finally found my father in the basement, where the telegraph was. It didn't take me long to realize his mood had changed dramatically from the evening before. He looked very upset.

"Are you sure? Check again!" he said to the telegrapher.

"I'm sorry, sir. Again — no news from Paris," the telegrapher answered.

"Your mother," Papa said, without saying hello. "I asked her to confirm when she left Paris, but . . . nothing."

"Papa, she probably forgot. Nothing to worry about." I did not have time to console him, although I wished I could have. Instead, I immediately asked for permission to meet my friends.

"All right, my dear," he said, trying to smile. "But Mr. Nelson will go with you. And don't go far away from him — understood?"

I hugged my father hard, forgetting that last piece of advice. Then I ran off.

I found Mr. Nelson outside the hotel smoking a pipe and asked him to find a carriage for me as soon as possible. Our butler was efficient, as usual, and in a matter of minutes we were in a small carriage.

I promised the coachman double pay if he managed to get to Carnaby Street by ten o'clock. He did his best, but the traffic was awful. He tried to squeeze the carriage through the crowd at the market on Carnaby Street. Since I was already ten minutes late, I decided I better walk the rest of the way. I paid him some extra money anyway and got out of the carriage with Mr. Nelson.

The colors, smells, and sounds of the market surrounded us. Despite the confusion, I immediately noticed a tall, but slouching young man, wrapped in a light wool cloak on the other side of the road. My heart started beating faster. It was Sherlock Holmes.

Even Mr. Nelson saw my friend and turned toward me, looking at me like he wanted to say, *Don't worry, I've got everything, Miss Irene. Just try not to get in trouble!*

"I'll be here waiting for you with a carriage at twelve o'clock sharp — understood?" said Mr. Nelson.

"Understood!" I confirmed.

I hugged the butler, not even considering the fact that it was probably not considered a proper gesture.

I was very happy to see Sherlock once again, and I wished I could have hugged him as well, but first we had to set something straight.

"Good morning, Holmes," I said. I made sure my voice was cold. "I see you managed to get some decent clothes. I'm glad! Even if that . . . vagabond attire gave you a certain charm, you know?"

Sherlock laughed, throwing his head back. "Welcome, Irene Adler!" he greeted me. "So you really did become all posh like I feared!"

"Well I couldn't have become very posh if I'm here now," I answered.

Sherlock didn't say a word. I saw wrinkles forming on his forehead, and I knew he was worrying that I was truly offended by what he had done at the Dover port. He opened his mouth to say something, but no sound came out. He looked so troubled then that I decided I'd had my revenge.

"What do you say we wait for Lupin inside?" I suggested. I smiled at him. "You can buy me something warm, and then tell me what you were thinking at the port!"

"Great idea!" agreed Sherlock, and he started smiling again.

We entered the Shackleton Coffee House, an old wooden cottage. Looking around, I saw merchants eating before going back on the road, ladies with bad reputations sipping coffee, and people who worked at the market lying on benches. Sherlock had promised me in his letter that he would take me to the most "disreputable places" in town, and it seemed that so far he was keeping his word. He ordered two cups of hot cocoa and grabbed two chairs.

"It's very simple," he began, handing one to me. "When I got your note that you were coming to London, I thought it would be nice to greet you."

"But how did you know that I was coming on that boat?" I asked, surprised. "I didn't write that in my message!"

Sherlock smiled. "I just needed to think," he answered. "That kind of trip requires a few days to prepare. Knowing that your father seeks only the best service, I knew that he would want to sail on the new ferry Northern Star, which does the Boulogne–Dover trip just once a week. Putting those two pieces of information together, I solved the mystery. Then I took advantage of a lucky coincidence. My mother had been begging me for months to bring some pillows to an old cousin who lives in Dover. For once, I was happy to help with one of her requests!"

We laughed together. I was happy to be with my friend and his curious mind again. But I also wondered where Arsène Lupin was.

In the meantime, the two cups of hot cocoa were ready for us. I immediately noticed Sherlock's ecstatic look, and he did not wait a second before diving his nose into the cup.

"It's delicious," I said, sipping the thick, dark-brown liquid.

"I don't like the taste," confessed Sherlock.

I looked at him in shock.

"I'm not interested in the smell. It's the effect it has on my mind. Cocoa makes me more . . . vibrant! Ready, sparkly — do you understand?" he said.

"I think so . . . it's like the effect that music has on me," I answered.

I described the extraordinary experience I had the night before in detail to Sherlock. "I am not used to this type of emotion," I said in the end. "Because you know . . . a good young lady must be continuously bored — even during war times!"

Sherlock nodded, then sighed. "Boredom is our biggest enemy. By the way . . . do you ever think about what happened this summer in Saint-Malo?"

"All the time, my friend. It was such an exciting adventure! I'll never forget it."

"I won't forget those days either," said Sherlock.

We spent some time recounting the details of all that had happened that summer in Saint-Malo . . .

finding the dead body washed ashore on the beach, solving the mystery of the man's murder, and discovering the identity of the Rooftop Thief.

"I wonder why those things cannot happen all the time!" Sherlock said.

I burst into a laugh. That was Sherlock Holmes at his best. "Mr. Holmes, you're a monster," I joked. "Crimes are like toys for you!"

My friend laughed and tried to defend himself, but our conversation was soon interrupted by a commotion coming from the street. We stopped speaking and looked out the window.

This is what I saw . . . or what I thought I saw. A young boy had stolen a woman's wallet and ran away. Another boy, a little bit older, walked over to the woman and spoke to her, then followed the thief, yelling, "Not to worry, Madam! I'm gonna get him!"

I held onto Sherlock's arm and said, "Let's hope he can catch him!" But when I turned to look at my friend, I saw that he looked like he was about to play one of his favorite games.

"Follow me!" said Sherlock all of a sudden, pushing back his chair.

My friend went into the kitchen and grabbed

a big knife. I wondered if he had gone crazy, but I followed him anyway. We went out the back door into a narrow alley. Sherlock started to run, like a tiger pursuing his prey, and I did the same.

He stopped suddenly by a brick staircase that led underground. "I'd let that wallet go if I were you!" Sherlock yelled, pulling the knife out of his pocket. The two boys lurked in the shadows. They were dividing the money! The older of the two tried to escape, but Sherlock pointed the knife at his chest.

"If you give me the wallet back with all its money and you don't make another attempt to escape, I will let you go without calling the police," Sherlock said.

The thieves exchanged a disappointed look and nodded. They put the money back inside the wallet and gave it to Sherlock, then disappeared down the alley. They looked back at us with pure hate.

Sherlock and I made our way back to Carnaby Street. The woman was surrounded by a crowd of curious people.

When Sherlock handed her wallet back to her, she looked surprised. "Thank you, my dear! God bless you!" she said, checking to make sure the wallet wasn't missing any money.

"Hey! He's not the boy who ran after the thief!" cried an Irish fishmonger. "What happened to that other guy?"

"He went to . . . fight other crimes! The boy has got *such* kind heart, you know?" Sherlock lied, and he found that funny.

And I was having fun with him. But then I spotted Mr. Nelson with a carriage. A clock on an old building confirmed that it was past noon, but I could not leave without first asking my friend for an explanation.

"How did you know that those two —"

"From their hats, Irene."

"Hats?!"

"Of course. They wore identical ones. It couldn't be a coincidence. It was more likely that it was because they had stolen the hats from some unlucky shop. An easy connection to make, don't you think?"

I did not think so, but I didn't have time to object. "I must go, Sherlock! Mr. Nelson's waiting."

"How long will you be in London?" he called.

"A week. I'm staying at the Claridge's!"

"Then we'll see each other again!"

I ran off, hoping it was the truth.

# Chapter 7

# DREAMS AND SURPRISES

I arrived at lunch out of breath and a few minutes late, but my father didn't even notice. He said hello to me like I was some kind of distant relative, without even asking where I had been or who I had met.

I tried to start a conversation, but my father gave short answers. He ordered a roast with steamed vegetables on the side and ate in silence.

When my father was done eating, he placed his napkin on the table and politely asked the waiter to take away his plate. He had barely eaten any of his meat.

"Listen," he began, with a long breath. "Your mother has not responded to the telegrams."

"Are you worried?" I asked foolishly. Of course he was. Everyone was. The news coming from Paris and the Franco-Prussian War covered the front pages of every newspaper.

"I'm going to get her," he said.

"And are you both going to come back here?" I asked quietly.

"Of course," he answered, without looking into my eyes.

Then he shook his head as if to shake off his worry, and pulled out a red book from the pocket of his jacket. It had a hard cover and a fabric bookmark. He handed it to me with a tiny smile.

It was a small and elegant tourist guide of the city, with black and white pictures of London's main attractions. On the page where the bookmark was lodged, Papa had written in small print by the text.

"These are the things you should see while you're here," he explained.

Only at that moment did he look straight at me, and I could tell by looking in his eyes that he had not slept well. "Will you promise me you'll behave for

Mr. Nelson? The idea of leaving you alone here . . . in a city you don't know —"

"Papa," I interrupted him, reaching my hand across the table to touch his. I felt his hand tense up under my grasp. After all, this serious businessman was not uscd to people being nice — and he certainly wasn't used to physical contact. "I'm not alone."

"I already explained to Horatio that —"

I kept my hand on his. "Mr. Nelson and I will be just fine. I mean it. Don't worry about me."

He nodded and looked away from me. Then he took his hand away and hid it under his napkin.

★ ★ ★

Compared to Edgar Allan Poe's stories, the guide to London was boring to say the least. I realized it that afternoon, when, while flipping through its pages on my bed, I fell asleep.

I dreamed. I remember it perfectly. My dream seemed to be based on the few pages I had read on the Tower of London and the people who had been kept as prisoners there. I dreamed of the performance from the previous night. I dreamed about Miss Merridew. She wore a white gown, like an angel, and she was running on a dangerous wooden staircase. In my dream, I was sure that it was the staircase at the Tower of London, even though I had never seen it. I tossed and turned in bed, upset but unable to wake up. In my dream, Miss Merridew arrived at a closed door at the top of the stairs and started to knock, louder and louder.

*Bang.*

*Bang!*

*BANG!*

The door wouldn't open. She kept looking behind her like she feared someone was coming after her. Then she saw him. She turned and saw someone who made her scream in fear.

I woke up. I was the one screaming. I had kicked the bedsheets all over the place and had fallen asleep with my clothes on. What time was it? Three? Four? I rubbed my face in confusion.

*Bang! Bang!*

That noise again, not far away from me. It was then that I realized that someone was knocking on my bedroom door. Without thinking, I ran to open it. And who was standing there but the curious Sherlock Holmes.

"Sherlock?" I asked, surprised.

"Were you screaming?" he asked.

"A dream," I quickly answered.

I saw a strange look in my friend's eyes, as if he had something important to tell me, and I was curious to find out what it was.

*What was he doing here? And how did he find my room?* At that point, I had not learned this yet . . . when you are dealing with Mr. Sherlock Holmes, it is pointless to ask questions.

Suddenly, I realized I was not at all presentable and, by instinct, I tried to brush my fingers through my hair and flatten out my wrinkled skirt.

But that was all Sherlock allowed me to do.

"Can I come in?" he asked me quite directly.

I let him in, glad to rebel against the etiquette my parents had taught me. "What's happening?" I asked him, leaning my back against the closed door.

He stopped near the closet and did his signature halfway turn. I knew this move quite well — he used it to observe the details of his surroundings. Then he held out a brand-new copy of the *Evening Mail,* a London newspaper.

"You can't even imagine," he said. His tone was

unusually serious; it immediately caused me to worry. I grabbed the paper from him and read the first page. Sherlock sat on the edge of the bed. As he looked around the room, he spotted the red guide to London.

"Good publication . . . if you're looking for all the boring things that you must *not* see in London," he said, smiling as he walked over to pick it up off my desk.

In the meantime, I read every headline in the *Evening Mail,* looking for something that would catch my attention. News of the Franco-Prussian War took up almost the whole paper, but I knew that was not what Sherlock wanted me to read.

"I don't understand . . ." I said, looking up at him.

Sherlock had opened the London guide and was reading it. Without even looking at the newspaper, he pointed at an article on the bottom left-hand corner of the front page.

I began to read. Alfred Santi, personal assistant of Giuseppe Barzini, the famous composer, had been found murdered in his hotel room.

I looked at Sherlock, my mouth open in shock. "When?"

"Last night. At the Hotel Albion."

I remembered the two young men from the previous night at the theater — Barzini's two young assistants that I had seen bump heads as they both bowed. One of them was Alfred Santi. A victim of a front-page murder!

I felt shivers move down my spine. But while it was a significant piece of news, it did not explain the worried look on Sherlock's face.

Sherlock considered murders exciting problems to solve. There had to be more to the story.

"And how did it happen?" I asked, suspicious.

Sherlock quickly flipped through the pages of the guide. "Finish reading the article," he told me.

According to the journalist, they caught the murderer. And it was a French acrobat, whose name was . . . *Théophraste Lupin!*

I stopped breathing. I closed my eyes, swallowed, and then opened my eyes again. All the letters were still there in front of me, lined up to make that name.

Théophraste Lupin.

My friend Arsène's father.

# Chapter 8

# A DARK TRUTH

All it took was a look between us, and without a word, Sherlock and I were running toward the door.

"Lupin's father can't be a murderer!" I said as we hurried down the red velvet stairs.

"I know," he replied. "Mr. Lupin is not a saint, but he is most definitely not a murderer."

Sherlock said those words like they were fact. That tone usually irritated me, but on this occasion, it made me feel reassured.

As soon as we got to the lobby, I stopped. I couldn't leave like that, without telling my father or Mr. Nelson anything. *My father,* I thought. *Is he already headed back to Paris, or is he leaving tomorrow morning?*

Sherlock seemed to understand the reason for my hesitation and pointed at a waiter-filled hallway, which led to the back of the hotel. "Let's go that way," he suggested, grabbing my hand. "So no one will see us."

I bit my lip. For a second, I stood my ground. But then I pictured the newspaper article featuring Théophraste Lupin's name. If *I* was in shock from that news, I could only imagine how our good friend must have felt. And with that, I dropped all my hesitation. Lupin needed us — nothing else mattered.

"Let's go!" I said, leading Sherlock through the back hallway and out onto the street.

"I guess you haven't become too posh after all!" he said.

When we got to the main road, a voice made me jump.

"Miss Adler!"

It was Mr. Nelson. He was leaning against the Claridge's entrance, chatting with the concierge, when he spotted me.

Sherlock immediately tried to disappear against a brick wall alongside the road. Mr. Nelson, with big steps that made his coattails snap, got to me in a matter of seconds.

"What are you doing here, Miss Adler?" asked Mr. Nelson, staring deep into my eyes. "Were you, perhaps, leaving the hotel without telling me?"

I tried not to look at him. "I'm sorry, Mr. Nelson, so sorry, but . . ." I waved my hands around as I tried to justify my behavior.

"Let me remind you that in your father's absence, *I'm* the person responsible for you. And I don't think I need to remind you that running around in alleys like a thief is not an activity fit for a young lady," the butler continued, his tone serious.

"I wanted to tell you, believe me. It's just that — it's not my fault!" I objected, my mind completely muddled.

"If it's not *your* fault," replied Mr. Nelson, "whose fault is it?"

He looked behind me, inspecting the street. I tried to block his view of Sherlock, but I knew I could only delay the inevitable for so long. I decided to tell the truth.

"It's Lupin," I said. "He's in trouble, and he needs his friends!"

Mr. Nelson pretended that he did not remember who Lupin was, but a sparkle in his eyes betrayed him.

"Do you have anything to add?" asked Mr. Nelson, peeking into the alley and walking over to stop in front of Sherlock.

My friend looked at me and shrugged. "I can tell you that I'm sorry," he said. "Or that it was some type of game, but . . ."

"But?" Mr. Nelson invited him to continue.

"What I really want to say is that I would never put Miss Irene in danger."

"Wandering around London alone isn't risk enough for you, young man?"

"Even if it's hard to believe, and I can understand why it might be, Mr. Nelson, London is a civilized city. So no — I don't consider wandering around here more dangerous than anywhere else in this world."

"Don't play games with me, Mr. Holmes," said Mr. Nelson. *So he remembers my good friend's name!* I thought. It was details like these that convinced me that Mr. Horatio Nelson knew me ten thousand times better than my parents.

"I'm not playing games," said Sherlock. "Irene and I just got bad news. It seems that our friend Arsène Lupin's father is in trouble. Big trouble."

"I swear that's true, Mr. Nelson!" I hurried to confirm. "We have to get to Lupin as soon as possible. That's why we tried to run away."

"And I swear," added Sherlock, "that I will take care of Miss Irene and make sure nothing bad happens to her."

"Do you swear, Mr. Holmes? That seems like a big promise to make for a young man such as yourself," Mr. Nelson said.

"I have nothing else to say to convince you, Mr. Nelson," Sherlock answered, looking straight into his eyes. "But what we just told you — it's the plain truth."

After standing still for a while, Mr. Nelson simply stretched one hand out in front of him to shake my friend's.

"All right, Mr. Holmes. Maybe I'm crazy, but I trust your word. I hope I won't regret it," he said.

Sherlock shook his hand, his face glowing. "You're

not crazy, Mr. Nelson, but you're a man that holds friendship in quite high regard," he said.

Mr. Nelson's eyes widened, and he tilted his head back a little. His reaction seemed to reveal that he was impressed by my friend's intelligence. Sherlock had grasped the essential point: friendship. Mr. Nelson looked as if he was wondering how that strange young man could have read his heart in that moment.

Mr. Nelson shook his head as if trying to chase his emotion away and, smiling, stepped forward to pat Sherlock on his back. I think I also may have seen him whisper something in Sherlock's ear.

"What did he tell you?" I asked my friend as we walked toward the Old Bell Hotel, where Lupin was staying.

"Nothing," Sherlock lied.

★ ★ ★

After walking for half an hour, we arrived at the hotel. We immediately asked the concierge to tell the Lupins we were there. After consulting some notes, he told us that the Lupin family was not in their room. The man wore a pompous double-breasted crimson jacket and talked to us like he was annoyed. That, combined with his heavy Welsh accent, seemed to bother Sherlock.

We looked around, not sure what to do. Finally, Sherlock went and sat on a couch in the lobby, where another person was waiting.

I sat down beside Sherlock and tried to ask him a few questions. He kept giving me vague answers.

It wasn't until later I learned the reason he wouldn't answer me properly. "I think that man in the lobby is a journalist!" he explained later, whispering in my ear. "God forbid that the press takes advantage of our research!"

After almost an hour of waiting, a young boy came to replace the concierge on duty. The person who was waiting with us began to pace around the lobby. Finally, the man went to the desk to ask the new concierge if the Lupin family was still staying at the hotel. He received an unclear answer — it seemed that the boy had no idea how to read the guest list.

The man cursed, paced in front of us a couple of times, and introduced himself. He was a journalist for the Globe, a famous London newspaper, and he was there for the same reason as us. The Lupin affair.

"If I'm not mistaken, you kids asked about them, too," he said, touching his mustache. He was a ruddy type — his cheeks were tormented by what looked like a rash left over from scarlet fever, and his stomach indicated he was a heavy drinker. "Do you know them?"

"Not at all," Sherlock answered before I could open my mouth. Then he gave me a look and pulled my guide to London out of his pocket.

"My sister and I are waiting for our parents to go sightsee," Sherlock went on. "We asked about the Lupin family just as a bet between us. We read about them in the paper, and my sister wouldn't believe they were staying at our hotel. Now she owes me a penny!" he concluded with a grin.

I nodded with a dumb laugh, pretending Sherlock was telling the truth. All of a sudden, a cold wind touched my ankles and made me shiver.

The man kept looking at us, as if to determine whether we were being honest. Suddenly, Sherlock stood up from the couch and grabbed my hand, as if he was eager to get moving. "Mama and Papa are taking too long! Always late! Let's go wait for them in our room, where we'll be more comfortable."

I followed him down the hallway in complete silence. But as soon as we got to the stairs and I knew we were alone, I began to ask him something. "Where did —" I started.

"Shh . . ." Sherlock interrupted, pointing a finger at me to make me shut up. But because of the absolute darkness in which we were standing, he miscalculated, and his finger landed on my lips.

We both stopped, as if a magic spell suddenly turned us to stone. That sudden physical contact caught us both by surprise. Just for a moment, my eyes met Sherlock's in dim light.

"Come on, let's go," said Sherlock, like he wanted to wake both of us up from that strange dream.

In just a few steps, we reached a crooked door that opened to the back of the hotel, and we felt the afternoon breeze coming in. We heard a few steps on the stairs.

"I think it's Lupin," said Sherlock. "I assumed, from the cold breeze in the lobby, that he, or someone else wishing to avoid the journalist, had decided to go in the back entrance."

I nodded. "Now — what room do you think he's in?"

"Seventy-seven, I'd say," Sherlock Holmes said very seriously. "Seventy-seven is the room on the top floor, so it's likely to be accessible to the roof — the perfect spot for an acrobat like Théophraste. I imagine that Lupin left in a hurry, as soon as he heard that his father got arrested, but I'll bet he's back there by now."

I could tell from the abrupt way he spoke that my good friend was just as embarrassed as I was about what had happened a few minutes earlier. We quickly and silently made our way to room 77.

"It's us," I said, as we arrived at the door. "Lupin? Are you there?"

I heard a couple of steps. Then the door opened, and Arsène Lupin appeared in front of me.

"Irene!" he exclaimed.

I barely recognized him. The handsome, tanned young man I had met in Saint-Malo that summer was now pale and skinny. He looked so fragile.

He welcomed me with a tiny smile. He hugged me, and the firmness of that embrace made me feel that what we had read in the paper was true.

He hugged Sherlock as well, but not the same way he hugged me. Then he invited us into the room that, like Sherlock had guessed, was just below the roof. I could hear pigeons landing on the gutter.

There was plenty of light coming in from two rounded dormer windows, one of them overlooking the city and the other one overlooking a street that circled the hotel.

We didn't waste much time chatting and catching up, even though Lupin tried to serve us tea, which Sherlock and I both refused. We were there to hear what had happened to Théophraste.

"It must be a mistake," Lupin started. "A big mistake. Nothing more — I'm positive! Don't trust what the paper says."

"Of course," I answered.

"They arrested him while he was on a gutter. It was near the hotel where that man got murdered . . . Alfred Santi," Lupin explained.

"Have you talked to him?" I asked.

Lupin shook his head. "They wouldn't allow it. But Mr. Aronofsky — the owner of the circus — and I spoke with a lawyer . . . someone called . . . uh . . ."

He dug into his pockets and found a business card, which he showed to us: *Archibald J. Nisbett, Lawyer.*

"And what did Nisbett tell you?" Sherlock asked.

"Nothing," Lupin said, sighing as he lay back on the bed. "I have a meeting with him in less than an hour to gather some information . . ."

"What a mess!" I said, looking at Sherlock. He did not seem worried, just focused — like he was thinking about many things at once.

"I have to ask you something, Lupin," he said in a firm voice.

"My father didn't do anything," Lupin told him.

"I don't doubt it, but . . . your father was arrested while he was on a gutter by the Hotel Albion," Sherlock said matter-of-factly.

Lupin closed his eyes, still lying on the bed.

"So the question is, what was your father doing there on the gutter?" Sherlock asked.

A long silence followed, interrupted only by the ticking of a clock. When Lupin finally started talking, his voice was so quiet that Sherlock and I could not hear him. Another silence followed, and then he said, "Fine! I'll tell you the truth. You're my friends, right? But you both have to promise . . ." Lupin hesitated, then sat up to look at us. "You have to promise you won't tell anyone for any reason."

We promised. I felt so many emotions then — pity, rage, shock — all of them bubbling up inside of me as tears threatened to fall from my eyes.

"I believe my father is a thief," confessed Lupin. Since neither Sherlock nor I said a word, he added, "I've known this for a while. It's the only explanation for the fact that we can afford this lifestyle." He gestured to the room around us as he got up from the bed. "Maybe it doesn't mean anything to you. It's nothing like your homes, after all. But when you're living on the road in a circus . . . this is pure luxury."

Lupin stood up and began pacing the room. "At first I thought it was my mother who took care of all this. She's rich, you know. And she's doing great wherever she is." He laughed nervously and shook his head. "Her family never accepted my father — they never forgave her for falling in love with a man who worked in a circus. Someone who lives on the road, someone not good or proper . . . a thief!"

He turned his back to us. The more he talked, the more he demonstrated the anger I had known him to have during the summer.

"That's how I grew up with my father and the circus. If I had to describe my mother, well, my memory fails me! But my father is more than just a father. You can't understand what it means to grow up and wander around with him and the others from the circus. You create a bond that's deeper than blood. My father taught me everything, and made sure I had everything I ever wanted. We followed the circus, but we always traveled on our own — first class, good hotels, first-rate locations." Lupin shook his head. "I've always tried to ignore where the money came from, even if I knew the truth."

I shivered, thinking about our walk on the roofs of Saint-Malo during the summer, and I started to think about what types of skills Théophraste might be teaching his son.

"Yes, my father is a thief. Now I've told you. And now you can leave this room and never come back. I can't blame you if you don't want to deal with a thief. But . . . even if it is true that my father is a thief . . . he is not a murderer. No way!"

I walked across the room and stood in front of one of the dormer windows so my friends wouldn't see the tears that were streaming from my eyes.

As I rested my forehead against the window, I noticed some of the hotel staff talking on the street below, and then I saw the journalist we met in the lobby taking notes.

I sniffed. Who knew what they had just made up about the arrest of the man in room 77. And everyone would believe it to be the truth.

There was silence in the room again, thick as the fog outside.

I could not take it anymore. "We must go to the Hotel Albion!" I said. I turned to my friends, drying the tears from my eyes. "Even down there, people are talking about Santi's murder."

Sherlock and Lupin looked at me.

"While you're meeting with this lawyer, Lupin," I continued, "Sherlock and I will try to figure out a way to help your father. What do you say?"

Neither of them said a word. That was the way it worked with us. Sometimes all we needed was one look to say everything we held in our hearts.

# Chapter 9

# THE ART OF GOSSIP

"Miss! Let me help you, please. Give it here, I've got it!" exclaimed the young Sherlock Holmes, as if the courtyard at the Hotel Albion was a stage and the laundry basket he held in front of him was a prop.

My friend seemed so silly and theatrical in his attempt to make good with the laundress that I thought she might promptly tell him to get lost. Instead, she seemed to fall for it. She let Sherlock carry the basket to the laundry room and took the opportunity to fix her hair and apron. I followed them, pretending to be Sherlock's sister.

When Sherlock reappeared in the middle of the steam that rose above the tubs of hot water in the laundry room, she looked him up and down and said, "Spit it out, come on! Who are you? One of those people who writes for the newspaper?"

"On my honor — no!" Sherlock said, pretending to be offended by the possibility.

"You're too good-looking to be from around here," the laundress continued. "You're too well dressed to be a busboy. So, if you're not one of the reporters from the newspaper, I simply don't understand what you're doing here."

"I help ladies in distress . . . the basic duty of every gentleman!" Sherlock replied, acting surprised.

"And who do you think I am, little prince? Do I look like a lady? And a distressed one, at that?" the woman asked, giggling. "It was kind of you to carry that basket for me, so I'll give you a tip in return. You should wear a pair of glasses on that long, pointed nose of yours . . ."

Sherlock laughed. The laundress laughed even harder and headed toward the steaming laundry tubs.

My friend followed her. "I don't want to lie to you, Miss," he began, passing a bucket to her. "The truth is — I live nearby, and when I read about the murder in the newspaper, well, I couldn't resist the temptation to look around."

"And you've done well, little prince," the maid replied. "If only I didn't have to do a darn thing all day, I should like to snoop as well!" She burst into thunderous laughter.

"Well," Sherlock said, straightening his back. "It's not every day a murder occurs close to your home. Not to mention one that involves a famous character."

"Was he really so famous, that man who died?" the maid asked, rolling up her sleeves.

"So they say."

"Psh! Those fools write like they know about things, but . . ."

Sherlock threw a sheet to her.

"But?" he prompted.

"But if they had met him in person just once they wouldn't have written that."

At that point, Sherlock turned and winked at me. The maid now seemed to have a great desire to talk.

"Interesting!" he said. "What do you mean exactly?"

"Well, the assistant — Santi? — he seemed to me a poor man . . . in spirit and in wealth. Now, the older one — he's rich and famous, indeed!"

"Are you referring to Barzini?" Sherlock asked.

"That's him, little prince. Not to mention Merridew . . . now *that's* a lady. And a classy one at that! It's true — certain things cannot be learned. I could spend a lifetime trying, but in the end I'm sure I could not even hold a glass with as much grace as Ms. Merridew does." She giggled, and then continued. "But regarding men . . . who knows. Maybe I'd also be interested in the grumps!"

"I'm afraid I do not understand, Miss," Sherlock said.

"I'll explain," she said, "but you must promise not to go gossiping around."

"I promise," he said.

She clicked her tongue, amused, and shook her head. "You're also a liar! At your age!" she chuckled.

"Not a liar, but, I repeat . . . just curious!" Sherlock protested.

"Then listen to me here, curious little prince," the laundress whispered as she threw a sheet into the water. "The fair lady Merridew was dating that man who died. Of the three, he was the least handsome and the most ill-tempered, and now the poor man is dead, God rest his soul. But . . ."

"But?"

"Well, the man's life must have been a nightmare! He was always nervous and in a bad mood, except when Ms. Merridew was around. Then everything changed. He would suddenly become cheerful and friendly . . . like a dog wagging his tail! But it never lasted long. As soon as she would leave the hotel to rehearse at the theater, he would become gloomy again. And he was unbearable!"

"But did he get along with Barzini at least? After all, he was his personal assistant."

"Don't joke, little prince! That man did not get along with anyone! Not with old Barzini, nor with the other one — the Frenchman."

"Duvel," I muttered, recalling the name of the composer's other assistant, who I had seen with Santi and Barzini in the theater the night before.

"He and Santi would shoot each other glances of fire!" the laundress continued. "They looked like two lions in the same cage. You would never guess that they ate breakfast at the same table!"

"And that thief who was arrested?" Sherlock asked. "What do they say about him, here at the hotel?"

"That he was also a Frenchman," the laundress replied promptly. "And he was apparently just a great bungler!"

Sherlock raised an eyebrow, inviting the woman to explain.

"To get caught by those fool cops who wander around the Albion area . . . he must really be an amateur!" she said.

"Your observation is not very respectful of Scotland Yard, Miss," Sherlock said, grinning. "But it is nonetheless interesting."

"What an honor!" she exclaimed sarcastically. "The little prince said that I was 'interesting'! Now, before I regret what I told you, either pick up a board and help me wash or get a move on!" she concluded with a final laugh.

It seemed that Sherlock wanted to gather a few more details on the matter from the laundress, but he was interrupted by a sudden noise that came from behind us.

We exchanged a quick glance and headed toward

the sound. It led us to the main entrance of the hotel. There we found a large group of reporters chattering, shaking their pencils and notebooks in the air toward the road.

A luxurious black carriage had just arrived and journalists were pushing one another to get to the front of the crowd. Through the mass of arms, I saw Mr. Barzini climbing down from the carriage, followed by Duvel. Barzini wore a brilliant dark green velvet cape and a top hat, which he took off in front of the reporters, passing it to his assistant.

"Let us by! Let us by, scoundrels!" the usher of the Albion barked, pushing between Maestro Barzini and the reporters. They shouted questions at the composer.

"Maestro! What feelings are you having now?"

"Mr. Barzini! Have you met Mr. Santi's murderer?"

"Could you ever forgive him?"

"After this tragedy, will you keep composing? Or will you also retire from the scene, like Ophelia Merridew plans to?"

"Will Mr. Duvel take the place of Mr. Santi?"

Barzini staggered through the crowd, shaking hands here and there. He had a bewildered air about him. Duvel, like a little dog, trotted behind him, holding Barzini's top hat close to his chest like a treasure.

"I have nothing to say!" the composer yelled from the hotel entrance.

But it was obvious that, on the contrary, he *did* want to say something, because then he announced, "If you must write something, write that Maestro Barzini lost someone yesterday who was as dear to him as a son . . . like a son!" Then he turned away, hiding his face in his hands, and disappeared into the building.

I found myself realizing, with some horror, that people seemed more interested in snatching a few words from the famous Barzini than finding out how things really happened in that cursed room at the Hotel Albion.

I was trying to make my way toward Sherlock, trapped in the crowd of reporters, when someone behind me called out my name.

"Irene!"

I turned. Lupin was running toward me. I met him partway and grabbed his hands, hopeful for news.

"So, how was the lawyer?" I asked.

Lupin was out of breath. He must have run half the length of town without stopping for a break.

"Let's sit over there," I suggested, pointing to a small café on the opposite side of the road.

"They set him up!" Lupin exclaimed after a long breath, his eyes fuming. "My father says he was framed!"

At that moment, Sherlock also joined us, and he immediately looked at his friend with concern.

"Get me something to drink," Lupin said, panting. "And I will tell you everything!"

# Chapter 10

# A TRAP

Lupin seemed a little less bewildered than when we had met him in his hotel room, but certainly not less concerned about his father's fate. So, while my friend was quenching his thirst, gulping down cups of tea one after another, I felt the need to find some words that could give him a little hope.

"Do you know what, Lupin?" I started out. "I think it's encouraging to notice that we have already discovered some leads that might help reveal the truth about what happened."

"Leads?" Sherlock repeated, puzzled.

"Of course," I said, without any hesitation. "Love, for example."

"Love?" Sherlock said, his eyes wide.

"A witch must have turned you into a parrot, Sherlock Holmes," I said. I was overwhelmed at that point, sick and tired of his skepticism. "Why do you keep repeating everything I say?"

"No, look . . . it's just . . ." he mumbled, taken aback.

"So let me continue," I said. "I am referring to the love between Mr. Santi and Miss Merridew. The laundress at the Albion told us about their romance. The great Ophelia has captured many hearts in her time. How do we know that some jealous suitor did not want to get rid of her new love interest?"

Sherlock looked like he was about to make one of his usual objections, but my recent outburst must have convinced him to remain silent. He simply shrugged in response.

"Or can we exclude the possibility that behind the murder of Santi there is his young French rival, Duvel?" Lupin said. "He will likely become the next assistant of the great Barzini . . . he had everything to gain from Santi's death!"

"No one can exclude him at the moment. But no one will accuse him either," Sherlock said, leaning back in his chair.

Lupin, however, smiled and looked into my eyes with great sweetness. It was his way of thanking me for my support, I think. Then he took a last sip of tea and cleared his throat. "There is another suspect in this awful thing," he revealed.

Both my eyes and Sherlock's darted over to him.

"A Spaniard," our friend whispered gravely.

Foolishly, I was startled. I suppose I was not expecting the appearance of a mysterious stranger in this story.

"Nisbett told me, actually, many things," Lupin began. "Taking Nisbett's advice, my father admitted some of his faults. He confessed that during the night of the murder he was really . . . working."

At that point, Lupin looked down at the ground and took a deep breath before continuing. "But that night he wasn't working on his own, like usual. This time, the theft had been commissioned by a mysterious man with Spanish accent. The man had approached him the night before in Brighton after our circus show." He paused.

SHERLOCK, LUPIN & ME

"And according to my father," Lupin said, "this Spaniard seemed to understand very well what he was doing. He had a very detailed plan in mind. In fact, he even mentioned a specific window at the Hotel Albion, and he explained to my father that that room was where a very cruel man was staying. A man against whom he wanted revenge."

"Such as killing him, maybe," Sherlock muttered quietly.

"No," Lupin replied stiffly. "The Spaniard's plan wouldn't have included any bloodshed — if it had, my father would never have agreed to carry it out for him!"

"We know, Lupin." I nodded. I gave Sherlock a diapproving look before turning back to Lupin. "Now tell us what this mysterious Spaniard had in mind."

"A simple but devastating theft," Lupin said. "He asked my father to steal a statue of jade while the room was empty. The statue was a good-luck charm that Alfred Santi never let out of his sight. The Spaniard said that his enemy was so superstitious, and so obsessed with that statue, that stealing it would have Santi at his mercy."

"Sounds like a fictional story," Sherlock said. "I do not understand how Mr. Théophraste —"

"Are you unable to believe this?" Lupin asked. "It's simple, Sherlock. The man was serious about his intentions. He paid my father a deposit of two hundred guineas, with a promise to pay the same amount after the job was completed."

Sherlock let out a loud whistle, which made all the customers in the café turn to look. It was, indeed, a considerable sum of money, and it explained perfectly why Théophraste Lupin was convinced that the matter was serious.

"Did he tell you, by chance, where they met up afterward?" I asked.

"This I do not know," Lupin admitted. "But I'll ask the lawyer tomorrow."

"All right. But now — part of the story is missing. The part where things go wrong. Terribly wrong," Sherlock said, taking his chin in his hands.

"That's right," Lupin agreed. "Here's what happened . . . my father left our room around one in the morning, convinced that I was sleeping. He went onto the roof, as always, but this time he never came back. He got to the Hotel Albion, climbed a

drainpipe — the one next to the door in the back — and entered Santi's room. Father told Nisbett that he immediately was suspicious because the window was ajar."

Lupin took a breath and then continued. "Soon after he entered the room, he saw a lifeless body lying on the ground. At that point, he followed his instinct, grabbed the jade statue, and fled, going out the window through which he had just entered. However, there were already policemen waiting outside. They must have been informed by the real murderer, who was pretending to be a civilian."

"A trap," Sherlock said.

"Yes," Lupin confirmed angrily, pounding his fist on the armrest of his chair. "The villain who came up with it did everything perfectly! And now if we cannot prove my father's innocence, and prove it quickly . . ." He trailed off.

At that comment, I felt a pang of anxiety. I turned suddenly to Sherlock, who nodded gravely.

"What is it?" I asked, guessing that the two boys had exchanged information that they considered not suitable for the ears of a young girl.

"As Lawyer Nisbett says, my father is at risk of

receiving the scarf of Tyburn," Lupin said in a faint voice.

"What's that?" I asked, alarmed.

"Hanging," Sherlock Holmes replied, frowning.

# Chapter 11

## THE RIVAL

That night, Mr. Nelson and I went down to the Claridge's restaurant pretty late. The long and intense afternoon made me somewhat quiet.

"Don't you have an appetite, Miss Irene?" Mr. Nelson asked me.

I stared at the broth in the bowl in front of me without really seeing it. "Not really," I said. "Actually, no."

"Did your friend deliver you bad news?"

"Oh, no, no," I answered quickly. "Nothing important. I am not worried about him."

"So, is this about your mother?"

"Maybe," I said, hoping my answer would put an end to the conversation.

"I know you don't want to talk about it. And I know how you feel," Mr. Nelson said out of the blue. He put his spoon on the table and carefully folded his napkin next to his plate. "I want to tell you something, Miss Irene . . . something that only your father knows about, and nobody else. A secret," the butler said mysteriously.

A server came to clear the table, and Mr. Nelson said, a little bashfully, "Thank you." Clearing the table was something he usually did himself, at least back in Paris. Then he went on, "Before doing what I do now, I was a sailor."

"A sailor, Mr. Nelson?" I burst out. "But you get sick during our journeys at sea."

"Don't judge, Miss Irene. When I was young, I was a sailor, and I didn't suffer from seasickness. But here is what I want to tell you. My days of sailing ended when I arrived in London and I was arrested due to an insulting accusation — that I had killed a passenger and had thrown her into the sea."

"You, Mr. Nelson?" I asked, shocked.

"I was the perfect culprit. I was strong enough to be able to drag her and throw her overboard, and I was poor enough that I wouldn't be able to defend myself against the accusation."

"Who was killed?" I whispered.

"A Prussian noblewoman, who, I discovered later, was traveling undercover on our ship. I worked room service, and for this reason, I was the first and only suspect. The police from the Scotland Yard arrested me right here in London. And they made a huge mistake," he explained. Mr. Nelson continued, "I certainly didn't do anything. In fact, that lady had treated me kindly. She was a wonderful lady, Miss Irene . . . a beautiful lady with a sad look about her."

I understood from the look he gave me that his story wasn't simply a test of confidence. But what I didn't realize at that point was that it was related to the mystery wrapping up my own past — about which he knew much more than he could reveal to me at that point.

That evening, anyway, he told me about how he was arrested and, briefly, about being taken to trial.

"I saw something strange, Miss Irene. I saw a man outside that woman's room on that first day of our journey. And when he saw me, he seemed very embarrassed. I had surprised him. He had a bundle, more or less this big." Mr. Nelson held his hands a short distance from one another, indicating the size, and then continued, "'It's very valuable,' the man told me when he noticed me standing there."

"Jewels?" I asked.

"It was everything the woman had brought with her," Mr. Nelson answered before continuing his story. "The man walked away quickly, and I knocked on the lady's door to make sure she was all right. I quickly realized that something had happened in that room. But I didn't ask questions. It wasn't my place to ask. She told me just one thing, 'Even if somebody asks, sailor, don't ever talk to anybody about this evening. Do not talk to anybody, and I promise that nothing bad will happen to you.'"

I gulped, asking myself why Mr. Nelson had decided to tell me about what exactly had happened that evening. And why now?

"Then I forgot the matter and even the woman, because the next day I was given another job on the boat and I didn't see her again. When we arrived in London, I found out that she had fallen into the sea.

The police arrested me because they believed that I was the one who threw her overboard that first and only night I met her."

"And what did you do?" I asked.

"I did what I promised her I'd do. I didn't say anything. I kept quiet, and I almost accepted the idea of being found guilty for a crime I had not committed."

"But it's unfair!" I protested. "You should have defended yourself!"

"Not everyone knows how to fight an accusation, Miss Irene," Mr. Nelson said. "It takes knowledge to do it. And in order to have that knowledge, you must have studied. It is easier to fight an accusation if you know how to do it." His smile was perplexing. "But I have never been alone in this," he continued. "I had a friend onboard — the captain of the ship. He knew from the beginning that it wasn't me. 'I know it, Horatio. Don't worry. Whatever the policemen say, I know it wasn't you,' the captain told me. He fought so hard to prove my innocence that he left the command of the ship to another captain. He did so much that in the end . . . he succeeded."

It took all my effort to keep from clapping my

hands. "And then?" I asked. "What happened to your friend — the captain?"

"To be honest, I don't know," Nelson said. "Many years passed, and we never saw each other again. I came to know your father, Miss Irene, and I accepted a position to work for him."

"And then I was born?" I asked.

"Oh, no, Miss Irene," the butler answered. "You were already born."

"Oh," I said.

"I told you this story because I know how your friend's father must feel. And I know that Mr. Lupin can count on you and Mr. Holmes. But this does not mean that you can take risks or do crazy things. I told you my secret because, if you need to, you can tell me about your secret, Miss Irene. You can trust me. But do not imagine that you will be allowed to do anything you wish to do, even if it *is* to help your good friend. I will not dismiss the obligations I have to your father."

I thought about that for a minute. Then I asked him, "Did they ever discover who threw the lady into the ocean?"

Mr. Nelson shook his head slowly.

"I understand, Mr. Nelson," I whispered.

"So, what are you up to with your friends today, Miss Irene?"

"We want to help Lupin's father, it's true. But we don't exactly know how," I admitted.

"Should I worry?"

"No. Don't worry, Mr. Nelson."

"Really? Can I trust you, Miss?"

"Yes. We won't take any useless risks," I answered. I hoped he would not ask Sherlock, Lupin, or me for a clearer definition of what we consider to be "useful," and that he would not want to know why Sherlock and Lupin were, at that moment, waiting for me a short distance away, just outside of our hotel.

★ ★ ★

Only a person who knew Sherlock at this age could confirm what I am about to say. The boy who would become one of the greatest detectives of all time has never had a strict moral code. He hasn't ever thought of things as "right" or "wrong," preferring instead to use the terms "possible" and "impossible."

It is for this reason, I think, that on that day he was chatting with the laundress at the Hotel Albion,

Sherlock didn't hesitate for a second to steal the woman's master key.

We went in the hotel through the back. We soon found that the inner doors were locked from the inside, so Lupin climbed the outside wall to a second-floor window that had been left open. He sneaked in a room, just the way his father had done a night before, and came downstairs to open the door for Sherlock and me.

"Come on, come on, come on," Lupin whispered, moving quickly up the stairs. "If they see us, we will end up in jail like my father."

Scotland Yard had staked their claim on Alfred Santi's room, where they had arrested Lupin's father. But the other two, the rooms of Barzini and his assistant, Duvel, had not yet been taken over by the police. We were most suspicious of Duvel, so we held a secret meeting in the hallway outside his room. We knew the room number because Sherlock, in the time that Lupin was gone, had pretended to deliver a package to Mr. Duvel.

"Let's try it!" I said, standing in front of the door.

I knocked. When nobody answered, I motioned for Sherlock to use the master key.

*Clank.* The door opened.

"Go," Sherlock said to Lupin. "If there is any evidence related to your father, you will see it first."

Lupin went ahead and nodded for us to follow. He found a light switch and flipped it on. "Long live the expensive hotels and their luxuries," he murmured.

Sherlock went to guard the staircase while Lupin and I looked around. He would be ready to warn us in case someone was coming.

Duvel's room was very messy. On the floor under the window, there was an open suitcase. The doors of the closet were open, and its contents were spilling out. There were some pegs in the closet where there hung strings holding dozens of sheets of music — music that looked as if it had been recently written.

"Do you know how to read music?" Lupin asked.

"Yes. I am taking singing lessons," I replied.

"And how are these?"

"They are nothing special, I would say . . . but I am not an expert," I said, looking them over.

"Duvel is not a poor man!" Lupin exclaimed, snatching a book from the ground. It had a small hole carved into the pages, which was filled with rolled-up bills.

"I don't know for sure what we are looking for," I said, taking the book from him and putting it back. "But probably not that."

"We are looking for a connection," Lupin whispered, going through the suitcase. "Something that could tie Duvel to my father, or to the Spaniard who commissioned the theft."

"Maybe a jade statue?" I dared.

"Exactly."

We searched the room for a whole hour before we heard Sherlock in the hallway. "Hurry up!" he warned us, throwing the door open. "Duvel is coming!"

"Let's get out of here!" I cried out, bashing into Sherlock, who was standing still in the doorway.

"There is no time!" he said. "It seems he is running. We won't be able to avoid him if we leave through the door."

Sherlock looked out the window. I started to panic. "I am not going out the window!" I protested.

"Then we don't have many choices!" Lupin turned off the light and hid under the bed. I followed him, and Sherlock ducked under the other side. We squeezed in the middle in order to avoid being seen.

I had my face in front of Lupin's chest and his arm was around my back. I felt Sherlock's bony joints on my back as well.

I heard Duvel's hurried footsteps coming closer, and then the key twisting in the keyhole. I watched his ankle boots move nervously between the door and the closet. All three of us stopped breathing.

Duvel seemed frantic. He kicked his suitcase and looked in the closet, cursing a lot.

It turns out he was searching for the book with the money. When he found it, he stopped cursing, threw it down, turned off the light, and left the room without closing the door entirely. I counted to ten and started to breathe again. I felt my friends doing the same.

"We must go now or we will lose him," Sherlock whispered, freeing me from a forced hug. He rolled onto his hip and got up, not even considering the possibility that Duvel might return.

It was then — right in the midst of that absurd situation — that Lupin kissed me.

I didn't even realize what was happening at first. He was embracing me in a hug, and I had my face pressed against his shirt, which smelled fresh. After

Sherlock slid out from under the bed, I felt Lupin stroking my hair gently, and I let him do so without fighting. In the dark, our lips touched lightly. They remained this way — I don't know for how long — until Sherlock called us anxiously, forcing us to come out.

★ ★ ★

Lupin and I didn't speak for the rest of the night. We were dizzy and stunned, trying to keep up with our friend who was chasing our suspect through the streets of London.

And we didn't talk about it later on, when other events and much more significant kisses were part of our memories. One thing I *can* say, even if I couldn't explain it . . . I never had any kiss better than that one.

It was certainly the event that I remember best from that evening, even if it wasn't the most dangerous.

"This way! Hurry up! We'll lose him," Sherlock said, moving like a cat through the darkest, most filthy streets in town. At first, gas lamps illuminated our path, but soon the well-lit streets gave way to wet alleys that were cloaked in strange shadows.

Noble houses in the fresh, Victorian style morphed into ruins and huts that gave off startling smells. The carriages disappeared, and suddenly we were surrounded by beggars passing through the shadows. They looked at us with hungry eyes.

"Come on!" Sherlock encouraged us.

We dove into the heart of the city and emerged in an area only few people had the courage to visit. The St. Giles neighborhood.

It was a place that carriage paths avoided. This neighborhood was far from any luminous lampposts. Everything was damp here, and mist hung in the air. Every encounter, every glance reminded me of the promise I had made to Mr. Nelson to stay away from trouble. I wondered what my punishment would be for lying to him so boldly.

Sherlock stopped at an intersection with his arm held out like a scarecrow's. "Shh . . ." he said. He leaned over a wall beyond which he had seen Duvel disappear. "He went in the front door," Sherlock said.

We all looked over the wall, protected by the darkness. The front door was elegant. The building must have been impressive at one time, but now it looked as if it should have been abandoned years ago. In front of the main door, there was a bonfire burning in the street, crackling noisily and bursting flames and grayish smoke into the sky.

"Who do you think those people are?" Lupin asked Sherlock, pointing out two shady characters standing in front of the fire.

"I don't know," Sherlock said. "But I doubt you go there for the pleasure of it."

"Wait for me here," Lupin told us just then. He stood up and walked toward the main door, which was guarded by the two shady men.

"He is insane," I whispered, watching him from behind the wall.

"I didn't know how insane," Sherlock Holmes said, crouching beside me.

We watched the scene from a distance, recreating it when Lupin eventually came back. First, Lupin introduced himself to the guards of that mysterious place, saying he had tobacco to deliver to someone inside. When they asked him to show it to them, he showed them a snuffbox that he had stolen from Duvel's room (yes, he had stolen it under my gaze, and I wasn't even aware).

The two men each rolled a cigarette, and then

allowed Lupin to enter. There were endless moments for Sherlock and me as we waited outside, asking ourselves if we should step in. But if the answer was yes, we did not know how to.

Just as I was beginning to think the worst, Lupin came out, said farewell to the guards, and came whistling toward us.

"It's just a gambling house," Lupin said, shrugging his shoulders as he approached us.

Despite the darkness, I noticed again the proud, fearless sparkling in his eyes that had struck me during the summer. And I did not know for sure if I wanted to slap him or ask him to kiss me again.

"And what does Duvel do in there?" I asked as we started walking.

"He's a gambler. He was watching a ball that was spinning around inside a wheel and betting on his money," Lupin said.

"Roulette," Sherlock said scornfully.

"No Spaniard. Nothing useful there," Lupin whispered, disappointed. "No darn connection to our investigation."

# Chapter 12

# NEWS FROM THE ROAD

The next day, Sherlock and I waited at the Shackleton Coffee House for Lupin to arrive. We had already ordered our usual hot cocoa when he entered the café.

Lupin had changed his clothes and put on a suit and tie. He was wearing well-polished shoes that made him look like a man — not like the boy I knew him to be. He had combed his normally disobedient hair back off his forehead, showing off his dark, sparkling eyes.

Two young ladies turned to watch him as he

made his way to our table and sat down without greeting us.

"It can't be him," Lupin said.

"Have you talked to Nisbett?" Sherlock asked.

"Yes," Lupin confirmed. Then he looked at me.

"What is the news?" I asked. I felt overwhelmed by a wave of energy, by the need to keep talking.

"From what it seems, my father was in a mess of a situation," Lupin said. "He keeps sharing pieces of information about what happened that night with Nisbett. I haven't been given the permission to meet him yet, but I will make it happen."

His hot cocoa arrived just then. He blew on it and sipped it slowly.

"And why do you say that it could not be Duvel?" asked Sherlock.

"Because it seems the Spaniard was quite tall —"

"While Duvel is short and skinny," I observed.

"Exactly." He paused. "After the crime had been carried out, they met in London at a pub on Baker Street," Lupin said.

"Which one?" Sherlock asked.

Lupin shook his head. "I don't know," he answered. "But let's go check. It's not far from here."

We sipped our beverages slowly and tried to calm ourselves again before heading out.

I joked with Lupin about a smudge that was on his nose, and I analyzed the events of the day with Sherlock.

Suddenly, I saw Sherlock stiffen. He stretched his neck, straightened his shoulders, and assumed his characteristic expression of a hawk, ready to prey upon any detail he could find.

*What could be going on in that mind of his?* I wondered.

"Listen! Outside," he told us.

I tried to listen beyond the noises of the coffee house, the clinking of silverware and the boisterous conversations . . . and I was able to hear noises from the street. The wheels of carriages on the pavement, horse hooves clomping, the brass horns directing traffic at intersections and . . . the voice of a paperboy on Fleet Street, the street where all the newspapers were sold.

"Special edition! Special edition! The famous singer disappeared! All the details for only fifteen cents! All the details!"

The paperboy continued shouting. "Special

edition! Merridew does not go to Buckingham Palace! The disappearance of the singer! A new mystery shocks the opera world. All the details for only fifteen cents! All the details!"

Lupin punched the armrest of his chair in frustration. "I hope they won't think this is also my father's doing!"

Sherlock and I looked at each other.

"Are you thinking what I'm thinking?" I asked in a low voice.

"That we do not have fifteen cents?" Sherlock Holmes replied.

★ ★ ★

The headline on the disappearance of Ophelia Merridew was more than the news itself.

The details were few and far between. The singer attended tea in the afternoon, but then she did not show up at the court. And she wasn't in her hotel room.

"She left while we were there," I whispered.

"Did she leave?" Lupin asked me. "How do we know that she left and that they don't have her?"

"Has she been murdered?" I asked.

I was hoping to hear Sherlock's opinion, but he was deep in thought.

It was as if he was inside a safe. He kept twisting the teaspoon for his hot cocoa between his fingers absent-mindedly.

"Do you remember how Duvel looked yesterday evening?" I persisted. "The man seemed crazy."

"As far as we know, Duvel had nothing to do with Merridew," Lupin answered. "On the other hand, Santi was the one who dated her, and who, of Barzini's two assistants, was the most —" He hesitated, and finally finished, "in love with her."

I may be the only one who noticed his hesitation when he said those last words. Or maybe — and this is more probable — I wanted to believe he said them like that to imagine that there was something between us, which wasn't the case.

It was inevitable that I would analyze these things Lupin said, because back then, and even later on, it wasn't easy for me to understand his real emotions. Sometimes they were so intense that they could be seen on his face, and sometimes they were so distant I couldn't read them at all.

I tried to help him. "The situation is as follows,"

I began. "In my opinion, there are three persons involved: Ophelia and the two assistants — Santi and Duvel. And maybe, when we discover what happened among those three, we can find out about the role that this mysterious Spaniard played in everything."

"But what about Barzini?" Lupin asked. "The three people you just mentioned worked for him, after all."

I shook my head. "Barzini is a man with a good reputation. And he does not need the other three as they need him."

"Not even Merridew?" Lupin answered. "She's more famous than Barzini. Look at the headlines. That poor Santi has been immediately forgotten, while she . . ." He trailed off.

I had to agree with him. The fact that a famous lady had not made it to Buckingham Palace seemed much more interesting to the public than the murder of the humble assistant of Maestro Barzini, Alfred Santi.

"Sherlock?" I asked at that point. "Are you still with us?"

Our friend looked at us distantly, then he gave his

body a shake and exclaimed, "Follow me!" And off he went, leaving the café without any explanation.

# Chapter 13

# THE PRINCE OF RIDDLES

With Sherlock Holmes leading the way, the three of us soon arrived at Fleet Street. Sherlock stopped in front of a brick building that was beautifully decorated with two small Greek columns in front.

The sign near the door identified it as the headquarters of the Globe, one of the most popular newspapers in the city. In fact, it was the same publication that the journalist worked for — the one who we had met accidentally in the lounge of the Old Bell Hotel while we were waiting for Lupin.

Sherlock pointed to a person who passed by,

asking him, without hesitation, "Is the editor here? I need to talk to him."

The reporter looked him up and down with the same expression as if you were at the market and evaluating a fish to see how fresh it is. Then, with a sneer, he said, "Sure boy, of course. At the end of the hallway, you'll also find Queen Victoria's office."

Sherlock Holmes did not allow the sarcasm to deter him, and he headed down the hallway.

Trusting that nobody took interest in us, Lupin and I followed Sherlock . . . that is, until we were stopped.

"Hey, you!" an angry voice addressed us. "Where are you going?"

A huge person appeared in front of Sherlock. His hands were stained with ink.

"To the editor's office," Sherlock answered calmly.

"What's this? A joke?" the person snickered. "And why would you three be going to the editor's office?"

"We have to speak with him," our friend answered, finally indicating that Lupin and I were with him.

"And is he eager to speak with you?" the man asked. "Hey, Enoch!" he exclaimed, calling to a friend on the other side of the hallway. "Have you heard this? There are three children who say they would like to talk to the editor!"

Enoch answered before coming out of his office. "That's a good one! Let's write it down for the satire page!" He then appeared in the doorway. "I've been trying to meet with him myself for three months!"

We looked each other up and down. It was the man with the pockmarked cheeks we had met at the hotel. "But I know you . . ." he whispered.

"Who are these three, Enoch?" the giant man asked.

"I want to talk to the editor," Sherlock persisted.

"You have, in front of you, his deputy," Enoch said, pointing to the other man.

"Could you tell me why you are making me waste all my time, you four?" the deputy said.

"The Prince of Riddles should not be treated this way," Sherlock said suddenly.

The two reporters looked at each other, then began to laugh. "Do not tell me that you have come here because you weren't able to solve this week's mystery."

The "Prince of Riddles" was a section of the Globe filled with puzzles and word problems to solve. It was published every Tuesday on the last page of the evening publication.

"It's me, the Prince of Riddles," said Sherlock.

The deputy's smile faded.

"Pff!" Enoch suddenly exclaimed. "And do you really think that we believe you, lad?"

"The riddles reach your office in an anonymous envelope each Monday evening," Sherlock said. "And the one you haven't published yet starts like this . . ."

In front of the increasingly bewildered eyes of the two men, Sherlock Holmes announced, word for word, a riddle about four men dressed in black who were running in the rain. "And the solution of the riddle is that they are all at a funeral," he concluded.

A long moment of silence followed.

"Gosh, lad!" Enoch said, scratching his head.

"Why do you want to talk to the editor?" the deputy asked.

"I need to talk to the best of your reporters," Sherlock answered. Then he looked behind him, into the noisy publishing house. "But not here!"

The deputy raised his eyes to Enoch. "The best of our reporters? All right," he said, sighing. "I'll grab a coat and follow you."

The five of us headed to a pub. The two men seemed frustrated that they had to give up their precious time to three children, but their skepticism seemed to dissolve after some sips of beer and Sherlock's shrewdness. Lupin's elegance and my red curls did the rest.

The topic that Sherlock was interested to hear about was Ophelia Merridew.

"I am sure you have unleashed your boys to discover anything about her," he began. "But we do not intend to wait for the next issue of the Globe in order to read what you've discovered."

The deputy bent over his pint. "And why do you want to know?"

"That does not concern our chat," Sherlock said.

"Just listen to the way he is talking!" the deputy burst out, loosening his tie.

"The Prince of Riddles . . ." Enoch reminded him, wiping the foam from his mustache with the back of his hand.

"Cards on the table, lad," the deputy said decidedly. "I won't ask you why you want to know about Ophelia Merridew, and we will tell you what we know about her. What will you do in exchange?"

"Well, I will keep on doing what I've been doing for your newspaper," Sherlock answered, drumming his fingers on the table. "There is some good competition here on Fleet Street . . ."

"Are you threatening me with your stupid section of riddles?"

Sherlock held his look quietly.

"In exchange," interrupted Lupin, who had not said a word until that moment, "we will tell you the name of the murderer of Alfred Santi."

"But we already know that," Enoch answered. "He's a thief . . . a scoundrel who works for the circus."

At that point, I predicted how Lupin would react, and I managed to stop him before he lunged at the reporter. It took all my strength to keep him sitting calmly.

"Hey!" Enoch cried, astonished. "What did I say?"

"Be careful what you say! Be careful!" Lupin addressed him with fire in his eyes.

"You are all mad, the three of you!" shouted the deputy.

Sherlock ignored him and continued. "My friend is telling the truth. We have information that has led us to believe that things happened much differently than what was published in the news."

"This is not unusual," Enoch said. "But the fact remains, the tightrope walker is in prison waiting to be hanged."

"He will not be," Lupin said grimly.

Enoch nodded gravely and then turned to Lupin. "You know him well, huh?" he guessed, finally understanding that there was a relationship between Lupin and the accused murderer. "I'm sorry for what I said."

"No hard feelings," Lupin said.

"Then it's settled," the deputy said. "Our information for yours."

Sherlock Holmes stretched out his hand across the table.

"And another year of the 'Prince of Riddles,'" the deputy added before shaking his hand.

"It's a deal."

Then the three of us got closer around the table, waiting to find out what the Globe had gathered on the case of Ophelia Merridew's disappearance.

"Actually," Enoch began, "what I know is not much. The most important news, which you might already know, is that Ophelia Merridew is a stage name."

I did not know that, but I did not interrupt him.

"Her real name is Olive, Olive something, and she was born in London. She grew up quite poor, apparently. When the singer became rich and famous, she moved her family to a remote place in the French Midi . . . certainly out of reach for a poor reporter on Fleet Street! All that remains of her past here in London is a ditzy, old aunt. Ophelia went to visit her every time she was on tour here. There is also a friend from her youth," Enoch pulled a torn, greasy notebook from his pocket. "Her name is Hortence. She's a talented seamstress, but other than that, we don't know much. I sent two reporters out to find her, but so far . . . that's all we have." He closed the notebook.

"It's not much," Sherlock agreed.

"They will talk about Merridew for a week more. Unless she turns up somewhere," Enoch said. "In London, luckily, there is always something new and juicy to throw out in the press."

After we found out a bit more information, we parted from the two reporters.

"You know what?" Enoch said to Sherlock a moment before we left. "Your riddles sell more copies than my articles." He started to ruffle Sherlock's hair, but at the last moment, he held out his hand in a gentlemanly fashion. "And it turns out that . . . you're a kid! But it's a wild world we live in, eh?"

## Chapter 14

# A THREAD OF THE PAST

The afternoon that followed was rather exciting. Before I got back to the Claridge's, we went to Baker Street, where Lupin's father had met the Spaniard after stealing the jade statue.

It was a pretty street lined with low-slung, brightly colored houses, but there was nothing that intrigued me about it.

Sherlock stopped in front of the house at number 221B Baker Street, looking at it with interest. It was there where the three of us agreed on our plan of action.

It was clear that there was a link between the disappearance of Ophelia and the trap that Théophraste had found himself in, but there were still many assumptions floating around.

Sherlock pointed out the possibility that there may have been tension between Ophelia and Santi. Maybe Santi had decided to leave her and she, mad with jealousy, had commissioned the Spaniard to carry out his murder.

I pointed out that I had heard the laundress say that Santi had been happy to see Merridew, so it was unlikely that he left the singer. Then Lupin said that maybe Santi was just pretending to be happy to see her.

"But some things you cannot fake!" I protested, silencing him abruptly.

We decided to start from where the mediocre reporter had stopped.

"Hortence is not a common name in London," Sherlock said. "And the tailor shops are almost all clustered around a street called Savile Row. With a little luck, we could track her down and find out more about Merridew."

"That's right!" exclaimed Lupin, hopefully. "Then

let's go. If she really is Ophelia's only friend here in London, maybe they have been in contact!"

Sherlock told me to consult the map in my guide to London to find Savile Row.

"And will you be coming?" Lupin asked Sherlock.

"I . . . I can't today," Sherlock said, sounding a bit embarrassed.

"What do you mean you can't?"

"My mother . . . she needs me . . . for an interview. We have to choose my school for this year."

I knew that Sherlock Holmes did not like to talk about his family, his brother, Mycroft, or his little sister, Violet.

"Choose a school?" Lupin asked. "My father is likely to be hanged, and you have to choose a school?"

"I'm sorry," Sherlock murmured.

"And I'll have to check in with Mr. Nelson, or there will be trouble for me," I said.

Lupin looked at us, and I read the disappointment in his eyes. "Do as you wish," he said as he buttoned his coat. Then he went off at a brisk pace without saying goodbye.

"Do you think he's mad at us?" I asked Sherlock. But he had turned his back to me, and was gazing at the building marked 221B with interest. So much interest, in fact, that he ignored my question.

"I like it here," he murmured.

* * *

Mr. Nelson huffed and protested, holding my two bags of clothes in one hand as we stood before the tailor shops on Savile Row.

"But do we really have to go in *all* the shops?" he asked with a sigh.

"If I'm not mistaken, you asked to look after me, is that not the case? Well," I said, smiling at him, "young ladies do this — shopping."

He pretended to believe that "shopping" was the reason I was dragging him on this adventure of mine, and he followed me into another shop.

"And do all the nice young ladies who go shopping ask every shopkeeper if they know a certain Hortence?" he asked slyly.

"If they are looking to find a certain person," I replied.

"And once they find her?" he asked.

"You know what, Mr. Nelson? You ask too many questions."

But at the end of the day, when I was about to lose hope, it was Mr. Nelson who found Hortence for me. In the last tailor shop we visited, Mr. Nelson asked about orders made to Hortence, and the owner wrote down an address for us.

"I guess we'll go there right now." Mr. Nelson smiled at me when we were on the street again.

"It would be nice of you to come," I said.

"You'll only go if I come with you, Miss Irene."

I stole a glance at him. He lifted the bags. "Now I'm curious, too," he said.

We knocked on the door of a private house two blocks farther down Savile Row, and a little girl only a few years old opened the door.

"Hello, little one," I said. "Is your mother home?"

A middle-aged woman appeared from behind the door. She had a beautiful, round face, big blue eyes, a small mouth, and brown hair tied back in a ponytail.

"Are you Hortence?" I asked politely.

The woman looked at me and then at Mr. Nelson, who smiled at her and said, "Say yes, please. We've spent the whole day looking for you."

"Looking for me?" the seamstress asked. "And why is that?"

"We are looking for Ophelia Merridew," I said softly, and I noticed Hortence move as though she wanted to close the door. So I added, "Do not be afraid, please. I'm not a meddler or a journalist. I'm just a fan of hers, and very worried for her safety. I know you were friends with her, and I wondered if, by chance, you have heard from her in recent days. Answer yes, so that I know she is fine, and I will trouble you no more."

Evidently that little speech that I had prepared and repeated in my head all day had the effect I desired, because the seamstress cheered up, moved away from the door, and invited us in for a cup of tea.

"In fact it is almost dinnertime, but . . ." she said.

"A cup of tea will be fine," I told her.

"Olive and I were born in the same month," the seamstress began, "and we shared the same difficult life."

They had grown up in the poor district of Bethnal Green, where, fortunately for Olive, the good priest of the parish of St. Mary had started a chorus of girls who sang in church.

"It did not take long for all of us to realize Olive's talent," said the seamstress. "And so one day the priest introduced her to a gentleman with whom he was acquainted, and this man was impressed with her talent."

"Do you remember the name of this gentleman?" I asked.

"Unfortunately I do not," she admitted. "But I know he was very rich and influential, and, above all, it was he who introduced Olive to Giuseppe Barzini."

"Got it," I said. I imagined that the mysterious gentleman who was very rich might have had a Spanish accent. "Go on, please."

"They went to have dinner in one of those restaurants in the center of the city," the seamstress reminisced, "where those like us dream of drinking at least a cup of tea once in a lifetime. Olive was very nervous, but the dinner went beyond our expectations. Maestro Barzini heard her singing and immediately decided to take her with him to Milan, Italy, to study, certain that she would become an opera star. Olive returned home to gather some of her belongings. And then we read her name in the papers. After a few years, her family moved to France, away from the misery of Bethnal Green. Can you blame them?"

"And Ophelia has never asked you to go as well?" I asked.

I noticed Mr. Nelson stiffen, just as Hortence did, and I realized that without meaning to, I had touched on a sensitive topic.

"Maybe for you it is not easy to understand, young lady. I can tell from your attire, and who accompanies you, what your social class is . . ."

Mr. Nelson nodded.

"But, you see, those of us who have less, more importantly, care a lot about our own dignity," she continued.

I bit my lip. "Excuse me. I did not mean to offend you."

"But you did," she said. "Unintentionally, of course, but you did. And so, that's how I felt every time my friend Olive offered me money to help out. I have never envied her talent or her success. I've always loved her from the heart. And I expected, therefore, the same treatment. I hoped that she wouldn't feel pity, but compassion for how I live."

I looked down. The small house that surrounded me reflected what Hortence was trying to explain. It was tiny and modest but was kept decent and clean.

I realized that our conversation was coming to an end. So I got up, sighed, and put forth my last question, "As far as you know, did all of Olive's family go to France? I've heard of an aunt who stayed in the city," I said.

Hortence nodded, leading me to the door. "Dear old Aunt Betty."

She said goodbye to us, but remained at the door as Mr. Nelson and I walked away.

"She was an old, crazy maid, who did not want to know anything about travel . . ." she called out, making me stop again. "But of all her family, she was the only one who really wanted something good to happen to Olive. She wanted Olive to do well simply because she was her niece — not because she hoped Olive would become the best opera singer in the world. And I believe that she is still in Bethnal Green."

Hortence closed the door slowly.

# Chapter 15

# INTO THE FOG

Bethnal Green was not included among the neighborhoods in my city guide. When I met Sherlock the next morning at the coffee house, he explained why. It was one of the poorest neighborhoods in London, he explained as we waited for Lupin to arrive.

After waiting for nearly half an hour, I started to wonder if Lupin was offended by the way Sherlock and I had departed the day before. But as we waited there for our friend, Sherlock and I decided we must continue to follow the trail of Ophelia's past to Bethnal Green, even if we had to do it without Lupin.

Sherlock had to argue with the coachman *and* pay the fare in advance to get him to take us to Bethnal Green. When I had settled in the carriage I asked, "But is it really so terrible?"

"Not in the sense that you imagine," Sherlock answered.

We plunged into the London fog. It was so thick that it even seemed to dampen the sound of horse hooves on the pavement. The pale sunlight gave way to a mass of uniform, compact gray. I noticed the houses become smaller and uglier, and then all I could see were pale shadows swallowed by the gray, wet, dripping sky.

The carriage left us at a crossroads, where Sherlock chose a direction at random. "Welcome to Bethnal Green!" he said sarcastically.

The only hint we had was a name — Betty. I looked around, thinking it was a hopeless mission.

"Let's try here," Sherlock said, taking my hand. We went into a tavern that smelled of rotten cabbage and tobacco and was lit by a forest of candles although it was still morning. It was little more than a big room with a floor covered in sawdust and a few people perched at tables like vultures on branches.

Sherlock tried to ignore them. He leaned against the counter next to some piles of dirty mugs. "I am looking for a woman," he said to the owner, who was a big, flabby man with a patch over one eye. "A woman named Betty — an elderly lady who had a niece named Olive," he continued.

The host kept on rubbing an empty mug with a greasy towel and repeated the question to his customers, who gave us hungry looks. I shivered, moving close to Sherlock for some protection.

"Betty, you said?" a bearded man asked while chewing. He had the aura of a gallows bird. "Betty? Perhaps it's old Betty who is living nearby?" He nudged another customer beside him, then added, "She had a little girl, yes! But then the girl left."

My heart felt as if it had jumped out of my chest. Could it be that we had a stroke of luck?

Mr. Scapegallows rose suddenly from his chair. "Come with me," he said as he passed by me. He stank in an unmentionable way. "I'll show you where she lives. If she is the Betty you are looking for . . ." the man continued.

We found ourselves back in the fog. It wrapped us in its cold, damp embrace once again.

Our guide muttered a few unintelligible phrases and led the way into an alley that seemed like a sewer between two decrepit buildings. "This way, come . . . this way."

We had just entered the alley when we heard the door of the inn behind us creak open again, at which point Sherlock stopped. "Run away!" he shouted.

Our guide turned toward us, pulling out a knife with a rusty blade. But he did not threaten us in time. Sherlock Holmes pulled a filthy beer mug that he had taken from the counter of the inn out from under his jacket and, pouncing on the man with the knife, hit him in the face. The man shouted, and his accomplice began to run toward us.

"Come! Quickly!" Sherlock grabbed my hand.

We ran away, quickly out of sight in the fog, turning in a completely random pattern through the alleyways and the little muddy streets. Following our instincts, we tried to get out of that hellish area, choosing to go down streets that seemed larger and avoiding buildings that looked as if they might crash to the ground. We slowed only when we were quite sure nobody was chasing us, and we leaned on the scuffed wall of a house, looking at one another.

"We were idiots," Sherlock said.

"Yes. That was foolish," I said.

He moved toward me, pushing the hair away from my face. "Are you okay?"

I nodded and then looked down.

"All right," he whispered, forcing a smile. He took a deep breath and looked around, trying to figure out what part of the neighborhood we were in.

"Do you hear that noise?" he asked me.

I paid attention. It was like the sound of coins clinking together.

We followed the noise through the fog and reached an old beggar woman on a street corner. She was playing with a few coins, dropping them into a tin bowl on the ground.

When she saw us coming, she looked up, smiled in our direction, and suddenly began to rant and rave.

"The devil is out there!" she whimpered, opening a horrible, toothless mouth. "The devil!"

She pointed to a window across the street. The milky, flickering light that came from inside was frightening.

Then the old woman grabbed at me, and suddenly my wrist was locked between her skeletal fingers.

"He has no face!" she shouted, pulling me toward her. "With his cloak and that hat from hell! He has no face! Only a big red spot! It's the devil!"

I found myself a few inches away from her wide eyes, and I let out a scream. Sherlock intervened to release my wrist from the woman's grip, shouting, "That's enough, old fool!" Then he grabbed me by the shoulders, hugged me, and led me away — far from the fog and the madness that seemed to hover like a curse among those decrepit houses.

We wandered around until Sherlock found a carriage. We hopped in eagerly, and Sherlock ordered the coachman to go to my hotel. I sat back and finally began to breathe again. When the carriage arrived at the Claridge's, Sherlock and I said goodbye.

I was relieved to sit down to lunch with Mr. Nelson. The waitress served me a delicate filet of sole with a side of golden potatoes. I could not help but smile, thankful for the company of Mr. Nelson, the news of my parents' return, and especially the bright, artificial light that shone down on us in that warm, welcoming, and luxurious hotel.

★ ★ ★

Later that day, I discovered that Lupin was not at all angry with us. We hadn't heard from him because he had received permission to visit his father. The visit had exhausted Lupin. A meeting that was supposed to last little more than fifteen minutes had lasted the whole morning.

That afternoon, the three of us met at the Shackleton Coffee House. I was very happy to see Lupin and hugged him hard.

There was an eerie feeling in the air. The city outside the windows of the café seemed immense and dangerous. Lupin's mood seemed to fluctuate between moments of genuine despair and near euphoria as he told us about meeting with his father.

He repeated, word for word, the conversation he had with his father. Only at the end, when Sherlock stood up from the table to order another cup of cocoa, did Lupin reveal that his father had given him a more accurate description of the Spaniard.

"He was very tall, as we know, and he was wrapped in a very long cape, with a wide-brim hat that hid his forehead and eyes, and a long, red scarf that he lifted up to his nose," Lupin said.

"What a striking image!" I muttered. "Did you hear that, Sherlock?"

Sherlock sat between us, and I invited Lupin to repeat the description of the Spaniard. As soon as he heard it, Sherlock's eyes widened in astonishment.

"Has he . . . has he really told you so? W-with those exact words?" Sherlock mumbled.

"Sherlock? What's wrong with you?" I asked him, alarmed.

He frantically pulled a handful of coins out from his pocket to pay the bill and said, "We have to return to Bethnal Green! Immediately!"

"Don't even think about it!" I said.

Lupin grabbed Sherlock's sleeve — or at least he tried to. But with a rapid movement, Sherlock pulled away and went out into the dim light of the cloudy afternoon, shouting for a carriage.

"Why does he always act like this?" Lupin asked as he stood up. "Couldn't he *try* to tell us what he's thinking before he departs at lightning speed?"

I didn't answer him because I was too distracted just then. "I'm not going back there," I muttered, thinking back to Mr. Scapegallows, the muddy alleyways, the bare branches that emerged like skeletons in the fog, and that madwoman who was talking nonsense about the devil on the street corner.

I had no intention of returning to Bethnal Green, but I followed my two friends out of the café anyway.

"Sherlock!" Lupin called after our friend. "Can you please tell us what is on your mind?"

Sherlock turned to look at us with the same glinting eyes that I had seen at the Port of Dover. "We need to find that woman again. The beggar!"

"WHAT?" I exclaimed. "Sherlock! You —"

He faced me. "Do you not understand, Irene? She saw him! He entered that house with the light flickering in the window. That beggar saw the Spaniard!"

I could not follow his reasoning. I shook my head in disbelief. "Sherlock, I — I mean . . . that woman is crazy! She might not even know her own name!"

Sherlock stopped a carriage with a gesture of his hand and went to open the door, continuing to look me straight in the eyes. "I'm not asking you to come with me, Irene."

I felt fear and pride fighting furiously in my mind. Pride finally won. I stared into the eyes of my friend. "There is no need to ask me anything. Let's go!"

# Chapter 16

# THE DEVIL OF BETHNAL GREEN

According to Sherlock, we were going to Bethnal Green in search of two people — the mysterious Spaniard and Betty, Merridew's aunt. But then, I wondered, why were we seeking out the madwoman on the sidewalk?

"The old beggar says she saw a devil, right?" Sherlock asked as the carriage passed over bumpy, muddy streets. "She described him in a very precise way . . . wrapped in a large cloak, without a face . . ."

"With a red spot instead of a face!" I almost shouted.

"And, in your opinion, do you think that would be the way a crazy old woman would describe someone with his face hidden behind a red scarf . . . like the Spaniard?" Lupin pondered.

"How do we even know the 'devil' that crazy woman was talking about and the Spaniard are the same person?" I objected.

"I'm not saying they are," Sherlock corrected me. "But they *could* be . . . especially if that lit window is the house we are looking for — Aunt Betty's house!"

I was struck by that possibility, and I began to look out the window eagerly. I had sworn to myself that I would not set foot again in that neighborhood — not for any reason at all — and now, a few hours later, I was gushing at the thought of returning!

Since those days, I have learned that adolescence is an unpredictable, reckless age. Anyone looking for evidence of this fact can find plenty by simply following my actions during those chaotic hours.

"Whoa! Whoa!" the coachman cried, stopping the horses so we could get off.

Sherlock passed him his last coins, asking him to wait in the area. The man placed a top hat on his head and smacked his lips noisily. "I'll wait for you for a few minutes, boy, but any longer and I'm afraid that someone might jump out of the shadows and eat my horses," he said with a wary grin on his face.

At first, the three of us headed off in different directions to try to find the old beggar, but before any of us turned a corner, we decided it would be best not to separate from one another.

We teamed up again, peering around buildings into the shadows and the dense fog that hovered on the roads like a small army of ghosts.

After a few minutes, I heard the voice of the coachman behind us, and then the sound of horses' hooves. "That fool is already gone!" I exclaimed.

But I was wrong. Soon the carriage appeared in the fog on the street next to us. "May I know what are you looking for, you three?" the coachman asked.

We told him, and he snickered, spitting tobacco onto the street. Moving forward on the streets accompanied by the slow creaking of the carriage and the heavy breathing of the horses was even more frightening than walking alone.

No light could break through the gray cloak of fog that wrapped up the houses. All we could see was the murkiness blanketing the streets and the tiny shadows of rats running away, frightened by our movements. The few people that we passed moved to the other side of the street with the same feverish speed of the rodents.

"It's here!" Sherlock said suddenly, making us stop. I could not figure out how he knew. We were at an intersection that was completely identical to the previous one, and there was no beggar crouched on the sidewalk.

"The smell," Sherlock said. "The smell remains." He crossed the street, put his hands on the moist, musty walls, and oriented himself.

"Over there," he said, pointing out a distant, yellowish glow. It was a window, the lighted window of a house swallowed by fog.

Sherlock ran in that direction. I tried to hold him back. I thought that maybe we should have a weapon with us before we went into the unknown, but when he shook free from my grip, I just ran after him. Lupin lingered behind, ordered the coachman to wait for us, and then ran after us.

The house was surrounded by a small garden invaded with weeds. It was short — a ground floor and an upper floor, topped by a roof with two chimneys. The lighted window that we could see from the street was on the top floor.

Sherlock pushed through the garden gate and climbed up the two steps to the entrance. The front door was ajar.

"Miss Betty?" he asked. "Ophelia?"

Silence.

Sherlock pushed the door open farther, making it creak in a terrible way. Inside, we found a true disaster.

It was dark, but we could see that pots, pans, furniture, and books had been thrown to the floor. There was a hallway straight ahead that led to a kitchen, a small library on the left side of the entrance, and on the right was a flight of stairs. A little light shined down from above. The railing of the staircase was damaged, and many paintings were now lying on the steps, their frames torn apart.

Sherlock put a finger to his lips. He made a gesture that indicated I should keep an eye on the hallway to the kitchen, and then he began to carefully climb the stairs.

I stepped over the frame of a painting, making the old wooden floor moan beneath my feet. I watched Sherlock move slowly up the stairs, one step at a time, and I stared into the dark kitchen ahead of me, my heart pounding in my throat with every step.

Suddenly, I heard the garden gate squeak, and I jumped. But I soon calmed myself, realizing it was Lupin who had joined us.

Then I thought I heard a noise upstairs.

"Sherlock!" I yelled. But he waved it off and continued up the stairs.

I reached the kitchen doorway and looked around. The first thing I saw were plates and cups thrown on the ground, broken into a thousand pieces, cabinets that were emptied in a wild way, and then . . .

My heart beat a violent blow in my chest.

I felt my legs freeze. A curtain of darkness fell over my eyes. I sat down slowly, unable to hold myself up. I would have certainly fainted if the cold of the marble kitchen floor against my legs had not helped me snap out of my nightmarish trance.

I took a deep breath and opened my eyes again. I was not wrong.

There was a woman's body lying beside the pantry door . . . white and still as snow.

I put my hand on my mouth to keep from screaming.

It was Ophelia Merridew.

The floor creaked and made me turn suddenly. I saw that Sherlock was most of the way up the stairs, and above him, at the top of the staircase, was an imposing figure. The person was wrapped in a cloak and wore a big hat pulled down over his forehead and a red scarf that covered his face.

"STOP!" Lupin shouted from the front door.

I heard a loud noise. The wooden railing along the stairway came down with a tremendous crash.

Sherlock Holmes had been pushed down the staircase by the devil of Bethnal Green. The force of his fall had taken down the railing, and he fell headfirst to the ground, landing in a pile of wood fragments and debris.

The devil came down the staircase two steps at a time, moving quickly toward Lupin like a huge black thundercloud.

I cried out in fear and ran toward Sherlock, who was curled up on the ground.

Lupin and the stranger scuffled. The masked man picked up Lupin and threw him forcefully across

SHERLOCK, LUPIN & ME

the room. Lupin landed heavily by the door. The stranger rushed out to the street, disappearing into the fog.

Sherlock was the first to get up, groaning.

"Are you okay?" I asked.

He nodded. He pressed his hand on his shoulder as he staggered outside.

Lupin followed him, limping. I found myself alone, just a few steps away from the corpse of poor Ophelia Merridew. I realized that the feeling of faintness I had experienced a few moments ago was still very real.

"Drats!" I hissed between my teeth. Gathering all my strength, I ran outside, stepping over the rubble that littered the floor.

When I arrived outside in the fog, I found Lupin and Sherlock both leaning against the iron gate. "What is happening now?" I asked, surprised by their calmness.

I heard the crack of a whip and a horse trotting in the distance.

"As it happens, we have given up our carriage to the devil," Sherlock replied. "So we have no way to follow him. But perhaps the coachman has seen his face . . ." Sherlock was turning it over in his mind as he thought out loud.

Sherlock stared silently at the dark trunks of the trees as if they were the bars of a cage. Lupin, however, was breathing hard. It looked like his temple and his right hand were wounded.

"Are you okay?" I asked him.

He slowly opened his fingers and showed me what he had swiped during the struggle with the Spaniard. It was a strip of red silk, a little bigger than a playing card.

"And you?" he asked me.

I shook my head doubtfully. Who knows? Maybe I was about to give up. Maybe I was going to confess that the whole investigation was too much for me. In truth, that is how I felt. But I did not say those words ever.

Just then, we heard a groan coming from the house. "He . . . help . . ."

*So Ophelia is not* . . . I thought. We all stared at one another in silence.

"Let's go!" I shouted at last.

And with that, all three of us ran back into the house.

# Chapter 17

# A PIECE OF
# RED SILK

"It's really amazing," Mr. Nelson commented as he leafed through the newspaper the next morning. "Half of Europe is in flames because of the war, and the newspapers continue to publish full-page stories on Ophelia Merridew!"

I broke the shell of my hard-boiled egg. Hearing Mr. Nelson say her name made my heart beat faster. I could not reveal to him that I had been involved in that murky incident, so I pretended to be absorbed in reading the first page. Thankfully, Mr. Nelson did not ask questions.

The Times reported that Ophelia Merridew had been found alive, but now she was struggling between life and death. She was being cared for in a secret place, because it was believed that she was still in danger.

Police had determined that it was only by some miracle the attacker had not been able to finish his work — to kill Merridew. They reported that until they received direct testimony from the opera singer, they would not have a definite name for the attacker.

There was no mention of the three of us, fortunately. Apparently, Scotland Yard was still convinced that Théophraste Lupin was guilty of murdering Alfred Santi. Nisbett continued to protest the accusation by insisting that there was some link between the murder of Santi and the attempted murder of Merridew — the latter of which, we all knew, had occurred when Théophraste Lupin was locked up in a jail cell.

My friends and I were certain that there was a connection between the two incidents. The dratted devil of Bethnal Green! But, as Sherlock said, at this point he was like a fictional character, a faceless and nameless ghost.

We figured it would be useless to try to talk to Nisbett or to go to the Scotland Yard. They would have simply thought of us as children who had too much imagination.

At this point, Scotland Yard had investigated Mr. Lupin's past, although not entirely accurately. They were convinced that he belonged to a dangerous gang of criminals. Therefore, they deemed that the attack on Merridew could have been one of Théophraste's accomplices attempting to muddy the waters, freeing Mr. Lupin of any blame in the murder of Santi.

A small sigh escaped my lips. *The investigators, I thought, wouldn't discover who the real murderer was even if he passed right under their noses!*

I finished my breakfast in a hurry and then stood up, ready to go out.

"What are your plans for today, Miss?" Mr. Nelson asked me.

"Oh, I don't know exactly," I said. "But I think I'll go back to take care of . . . fabrics."

He opened his eyes wide. It was clear he didn't want to spend another afternoon winding his way from one tailor shop to another on Savile Row.

"Do you want to come with me?" I asked anyway.

"Only if it involves something very dangerous, Miss. Something that absolutely requires my protection!" the butler joked.

"Then you can stay here in comfort, my good Horatio Nelson," I said as I got up from the table and smiled at him. "It will be an affair of refined matters . . . *haute couture!*"

I crossed the dining room, laughing the entire way. I pushed through the Claridge's revolving door and headed outside toward Sherlock's house.

The Holmes residence in London was simple, but had a great perk — a toolshed in the backyard.

Sherlock had made the toolshed his own kingdom, and it was there where he greeted Lupin and me that morning between screwdrivers, hammers, and saws hanging on old rusty nails; a massive workbench; and an unknown number of drafts in the woodwork that the young Holmes would have to mend before winter.

That morning, I discovered that the magnifying glass that would become Sherlock's famous tool belonged to, in fact, his older brother, Mycroft.

But it was that morning, Sherlock claimed, that he became the first one to use the lens.

Sherlock put on a pair of white gloves (which also belonged to his brother). He then picked up the piece of red cloth that Lupin had snatched from the devil of Bethnal Green and bent over to study it with great care. Seeing Sherlock stooped in that way, with his eye grotesquely magnified by the lens, made me think of the famous hunchback of Notre-Dame, and I burst into laughter.

"And what's wrong now?" he asked me, lowering the lens for a moment in astonishment.

"Forget it, Quasimodo," I joked. "Tell us what you see."

That day I witnessed the great detective's first investigation with a magnifying glass — with the very lens he would often be pictured with many years later.

But since I want to be honest about how things really took place, well . . . I must say that in the beginning, Sherlock Holmes's work with the lens was not very impressive.

"It is silk!" Sherlock announced. And then he added, "Valuable silk!"

Mocking him, Lupin made a shocked expression, and I had to try my hardest to hold in my laughter.

Sherlock, who was intensely concentrated on his inspection work, took no notice of the teasing and kept sharing his observations with us. "It is certainly not a piece of a scarf. It looks like a piece of the lining of a coat. And here . . . here are the initials sewn on the fabric! Three characters: W & R!"

At that, he put the lens down triumphantly.

"Is that it?" Lupin asked. "W & R could be anything."

"Not anything," Sherlock pointed out. "Indeed, it could be an abbreviation for thousands of names. But I can hardly believe the man is a Spaniard . . . considering that the letter *W* is extremely rare in the Spanish language."

"Good point," Lupin agreed.

"And that's not all! Wait here a minute, please."

He gave us the cloth and the lens and ran out of the toolshed, heading toward his house.

Sherlock returned shortly with a fancy coat belonging to Mycroft.

He showed us how the silk was applied to the lining of Mycroft's coat, convincing us even more that what we had in hand was, indeed, a piece of silk that Lupin had ripped off of the Spaniard's coat.

"As I have already told you," Sherlock added, "my brother is determined to pursue a career in politics, and it is for this reason that Mother gave him my father's good coat."

It was the first time that Sherlock mentioned his father, Siger, whose sad story I didn't learn until later.

"Now," young Holmes continued, "please smell the lining of this coat and then smell the scrap that Lupin tore off of the Spaniard's coat. Try to sharpen your senses. Smell, if you can, beyond the stench of the people who have worn these fabrics. Concentrate on the aroma of the silk, so to speak."

Intrigued, I tried to do as he said. The silk of the two liners did have, at their depths, a similar fragrance. "Aromatic!" I exclaimed. "Almost spicy."

"Excellent!" Sherlock approved, snapping his fingers in satisfaction. "The two fabrics have the same unmistakable smell of Indian silk, coming from the colonies of Her Majesty the Queen of England."

Lupin crossed his legs on his stool. "Then although he is likely a Spaniard, we know he bought his clothes here in England."

"Exactly. And we also know he spent more than a little on whatever this tiny scrap came from — likely a coat," Sherlock added, holding up the piece of silk with a grin on his face.

Lupin tugged nervously at his chin. Every little analysis or discovery, which for Sherlock and me may have seemed a simple move to solve a difficult puzzle, represented for Lupin, in reality, a step toward his father's freedom.

"And now that we have these letters, and we know that this silk is made in England?" I asked.

"Should we go back to Savile Row?" Sherlock suggested.

I shook my head. "Not quite Savile Row, but almost."

★ ★ ★

As soon as Hortence left her house, I caught up with her along the street, leaving Lupin and Sherlock hidden behind a tree.

"Miss Hortence! Miss Hortence, excuse me!"

The seamstress stopped to see who was calling, but as soon as she recognized me, her expression turned rather sour.

"Have you read about Ophelia?" I asked, moving toward her.

Hortence said yes, adding that the accounts were terrible. She walked slowly but steadily, and held a couple of jackets wrapped in blue tissue paper under her arms.

"What do you want from me this time, young lady?" she asked.

"Instead of being happy that your friend has been found, you seem angry with me, Miss Hortence," I pointed out.

"I find it a strange coincidence . . . you come to my house with your butler, both of you weighed down by packages," she replied, then she paused, as if to emphasize that she considered it entirely inappropriate to reveal the fact that I had someone in my service. "You ask me about Olive's family, I tell you about Aunt Betty, and then, the next day . . . then my poor friend is found right in the old house of this aunt — more dead than alive!"

"I do not see how you can think that I —" I started.

"I do not think anything, young lady! But I don't understand why you're here now," the seamstress concluded, nervously clutching her bundle of clothes.

"Because you are the only person who can

help me," I admitted. And then I told her, trying to be as honest as possible, that I was doing a small investigation into the incident.

I explained that we had a valid suspect that we believed had attacked Ophelia in her aunt's house, and that it could very well be the same person who had murdered Alfred Santi.

"It just so happens that I have a friend, Miss. And right now she is lying in bed and fighting for her life. So I hope that I do not hurt your feelings, but I will tell nothing more," the seamstress said.

"All right, Miss Hortence," I said, nodding. "I won't ask you anything more about Ophelia. However, what I would ask of you is your expert opinion!"

I was hoping that the initials on the cloth, W & R, would awaken some memory linked to Hortence's childhood — and therefore to Ophelia's.

So, without hesitation, I waved the piece of red silk before her eyes. Hortence looked at it and then looked at me like I was crazy. "What is this? A joke?"

"What can you say of it?" I asked, choosing to ignore her skepticism.

"It is silk. Of the best quality," she replied, examining the fragment.

"It is signed with the initials W & R. Do they mean anything to you?" I asked.

The woman paused to think. "No, I'm sorry. Not at all."

I bit my lip. "Could they be the initials of a tailor's shop?" I persisted, determined not to leave empty-handed.

"W & R?" Hortence repeated, pausing to think again, this time a little longer. "No. There is no tailor's shop that has those initials. Not on Savile Row, at least."

"Maybe a tailor's shop that has closed?" I kept at it, although I had less and less hope. "Or are there any shops that have changed ownership?"

"I've been here for a lifetime," Hortence said, "and I can assure you that I have mended a lot of clothes, old and new. I've never seen anything from your imaginary tailor, W & R! And now, with your permission, I have to finish my deliveries."

"Very well. I am staying at the Claridge's," I said. "If you think of something, or change your mind —"

"I have nothing more to say to you, young lady. Good day!" Hortence said, walking briskly away. I walked back toward my two friends.

"Now what?" Lupin and Sherlock asked when I returned to them.

"A waste of time," I said, disappointed. "According to Hortence, there is no tailor's shop that has those initials."

"We didn't need this," Lupin said, looking frustrated. "It could be a cloth that has been produced in the United States, France — anywhere else but here!"

Sherlock was disappointed. His theory — that the Spaniard's shawl was from England — was not looking as likely now.

For the umpteenth time since we had started that investigation, we were stuck.

I began to think maybe we weren't skilled enough to conduct such a demanding investigation . . . and maybe we would have to ask for help.

★ ★ ★

I stared at Mr. Nelson throughout dinner that night, continually asking myself if I should tell him about our investigation. I was waiting for the right time, but the moment never came.

Back then, it seemed to me that discussing our

work with an adult would mean betraying the spirit of our group.

"There is good and bad news, Miss Irene," Mr. Nelson told me in the middle of the dinner. "The good news is that your father let us know by telegram that your mother is doing well and that tomorrow or the day after, they will leave to meet you here in London."

"And the bad?" I asked, slightly worried.

"Perhaps, among your many thoughts, you have wondered what my job here is, apart from making sure you are safe and keeping track of your questionable friends, while your father has been gone."

"Actually, I haven't, Mr. Nelson," I admitted.

"Well, he asked me to look for an apartment rental here for all of you, and myself," Mr. Nelson replied.

My eyes widened. "We are leaving Paris?"

"For some time, it would seem so, Miss Irene. I'm really sorry . . ." and here Horatio Nelson went beyond his call of duty, displaying a fake regretful grimace worthy of a Shakespearean actor. "At the thought of all the distinguished Parisian friends you must give up, instead of spending goodness knows how many months in this new city, where you know only Mr. Holmes and Mr. Lupin. Those two will be barely enough to distract you while things on the continent are sorted out."

I kissed him on the forehead, which left him speechless, and ran happily around the room, imagining the moment when I would tell my two friends the news.

Then, when the excitement passed, I decided to keep the news to myself for the time being . . . at least until we saved Théophraste Lupin from the gallows.

★ ★ ★

I took a long bath, during which I let myself dream a thousand fantasies about my future in London, and when I returned to my room, ready to sleep, I noticed that someone had slid a thin white envelope under the door.

I picked it up and turned it over. There was my name and the address of the hotel written by a light and very accurate hand. I opened the envelope and there I found a short note, full of erasures.

*Dear Miss Adler,*

*I'm sorry about this afternoon, but as you may have guessed by now, I have difficulty trusting other people. However, I think I can fix that — at least partially. Thinking back to the piece of red silk, I finally managed to remember something. And now I am certain that the shop you're looking for is Wallace & Renfurm, not very far from Covent Garden. The reason why I did not remember immediately is because it is a very specialized shop, which only handles costumes — especially those for the Royal Opera House. Hoping to have been of some help. I offer my respectful greetings.*

*— Miss Hortence Cheepnis*

The tailor of the costumes for the Opera House in London.

We had a new lead!

# Chapter 18

# THE MAGIC OF
# THE THEATER

The Royal Opera House was closed, but fans had been visiting the theater frequently in the days since Ophelia went missing. People had lit dozens of candles in prayer and left them burning at the entrance. On the lawn were hundreds of notes that wished Ophelia a speedy recovery and only a few expressing their mourning of poor Alfred Santi, whose death seemed to have already been forgotten.

Sherlock, Lupin, and I walked around the entire building looking for a way to enter. The fact that the mysterious Spaniard was wearing a costume made

187

by the tailor Wallace & Renfurm convinced us that we had to look for the criminal among the singers, musicians, and employees of the theater.

Among those suspects, we knew we had to consider Henri Duvel, Barzini's French assistant, although his stature did not match that of the Spaniard. We concluded that Duvel could have hired someone else to play that evil part for him.

Walking around the theater, we heard music coming from some low windows that were protected on the outside by iron bars. We heard a piano . . . timpani rolls.

"They're rehearsing," I said.

This meant that one of the musicians would have to come out of the building eventually. But from where?

"As soon as someone comes out, we try to go inside," Sherlock said. "And if he doesn't want to cooperate . . . we will try to convince him!"

He pulled from his pocket the bag of shillings he had earned as "Prince of Riddles" and suggested we divide them among us in case we had the opportunity to bribe someone to let us in.

But Lupin objected. "Do I have to remind you

why we are here?" he asked, insisting he use his own savings for the cause.

In the end, we agreed that we should each contribute equal parts should we find ourselves in such a situation.

The three of us then spread out around the building, but made sure that we could still see each other from where we were posted.

Nothing happened for more than an hour. Then, after a good half of the morning had passed, a little man in a gray suit walked up to the front doors of the theater, which were on the side Lupin was guarding.

Lupin alerted us with a whistle. We surrounded the man just before he could put the key in the lock.

He glanced over us, alarmed, looking nervously from one of us to another like a fish caught in a net.

"Well! May I ask what you want?" he asked us sharply.

"Excuse me, sir . . . we have a simple request. Could you let us into the theater with you?" Sherlock asked.

"We assure you that it will be only for a minute!" Lupin said.

"Please!" I added.

The man began bouncing and nervously tapping his feet on the ground like a crazy dancer.

"Get out! Get out! Go away! The theater is closed, as you well know!" he yelled.

I touched his arm with one hand, and he suddenly stopped, surprised. "Please! I dream of becoming a singer . . . and I've never seen a great theater before!" I lied.

"And he plays the violin," Lupin added, pointing at Sherlock.

"And you?" the little man in gray asked him. "What do you know how to do?"

"Me?" Lupin improvised. "I want to become a costume designer, and dress up the most beautiful women in the world!"

"Pah!" the man said, not at all impressed, trying to make his way through us to the door.

"Listen!" I pressed him. "Have you ever heard of Wallace & Renfurm?" I asked.

To that question, the man raised his eyes impatiently. "This then! Three amateurs sent by a competitor to snoop! Is there anything they *wouldn't* do nowadays?" he exclaimed. "Never mind that! You made a bad guess. Costumes are not my business."

"Well, surely you must know if Wallace & Renfurm supplies for the theater at least!" Lupin burst out.

At that point, the man forcefully knocked three times on the locked door and then stood watching us for a moment.

"*Everybody* knows this, young man," he directed at Lupin. "Everything that's down there," the man went on as he looked toward the ground, "is made by them."

"Down there?" Lupin repeated.

"In the basement — where the wardrobe is kept," the man replied.

"Do you keep them all there?" I asked.

"All except the ones that are past their prime, wrinkled or faded or frayed," the man said, raising his chin. "And then they are given to performers less prestigious than those who work here at the Royal Opera House."

We exchanged an understanding glance. We knew, thanks to Lupin, that the Spaniard's coat was not crumpled at all, and that, if our assumptions were correct, it would have come right from the wardrobe of this theater.

"And there isn't any possibility that you could show us this wardrobe?" I asked, hopeful.

The little man in gray smiled pleasantly at us. "Sure, why not? But first I would like to introduce you to two of my good friends!"

At that moment, the door to the theater opened, and two quite scary-looking thugs appeared in the doorway.

"Have you called us, boss?" one of them asked.

"It must be our lucky day, Jack. We have a singer, an up-and-coming costume designer, and one who aspires to be the next Paganini! Where are you at with taking down the sets? Do you need to warm up your muscles a little?" the small man in gray asked them, chuckling.

The two big men rolled up their sleeves, each revealing forearms that were as thick as the ropes on a ship, and prepared to grab us.

"Just a second," Sherlock muttered then, putting himself between the men and me. "I think there is a misunderstanding, Mr. . . ."

"Collins," the man said, adjusting his round glasses on his little pig eyes, as if he had expected to be recognized.

"COLLINS?" Lupin leaped in enthusiastically, making me seriously fear that he had lost his mind. "Are you really Wilkie Collins? Wilkie Collins . . . the writer?" he bumbled.

The little man looked at him with curiosity.

"Writer, journalist, and playwright," he specified. "As well as an assistant to and friend of Charles Dickens."

"Charles Dickens!" I exclaimed. "What a wonderful writer!"

Wilkie Collins could not hide a grimace of annoyance. "I regret to inform you that he died three months ago, Miss."

"Oh . . . I'm sorry," I muttered.

"England has lost one of its best writers . . ." Wilkie Collins said with a false sigh. It was obvious that the event had not upset him very much.

"But I read your book *The Moonstone,* sir," Lupin quipped. "It is simply gorgeous."

"Are you being serious, young man?" Wilkie Collins asked.

"Of course!" Lupin insisted. Then he looked at me. "Irene, don't you remember? I told you about it!"

I opened my mouth for a split second before I

realized what he was doing. "Oh, of course!" I finally said. "It's that book you devoured in a single day!"

The little man adjusted his glasses on his nose. "In a single day!" he repeated smugly. At that point, he gestured at the two thugs to back off.

"Without even stopping to eat, sir," Lupin said triumphantly. Then he added, almost in a whisper, "Anything but Dickens. Quite frankly, sir, his novels bore me to death."

The little man named Wilkie Collins looked indecisively at the small group of people around him.

"Do you still want me to do something about these kids, boss?" the beast named Jack asked.

"No, no . . ." Wilkie Collins stammered, raising both his hands. "Never mind. The boy here —"

Lupin asked, "Could I have your autograph, sir?"

The writer felt his waistcoat, looking for a pen, and then looked into the pocket of his gray jacket. "Of course! I . . . I thought I might even have a copy of . . . but where . . . where did I put it?"

"Mr. Collins," said Lupin, grabbing his arm. "The autograph does not matter. But it would be an incredible honor for me to visit the theater with you. Tell me! Are you planning a new work yet?"

The writer waved his hands, confused. "Yes, something like that, perhaps even with Maestro Barzini. We have an idea from an old story of mine that has not yet been published."

"An unpublished one?" Lupin asked excitedly.

Nothing else was necessary. Softened by the effusive compliments of our French friend, Wilkie Collins (whoever that was!) opened the doors to the Royal Opera House, which led us right to the stage.

At first, however, our mission did not go very well. In addition to the employees there to take down the sets and some musicians there to practice, there were also some agents from the Scotland Yard in the theater, which made any attempt to look around impossible.

Lupin and I left the theater after just a quick tour of the stage and the orchestra pit. At some point during our tour, Collins had stopped to talk to Maestro Barzini and seemed to have forgotten our presence. And Sherlock, meanwhile, managed to disappear during the tour without Lupin or me noticing. One moment he was behind me, the next he was gone.

We were led to the door by one of the officers in

charge of interviewing the members of the theater company. Given the unexplainable absence of our friend Sherlock Holmes, we did not protest too much and allowed them to show us to the exit.

Once outside, Lupin and I searched for a bench and debated what we should do next. Not that we had much choice.

"We wait for him," I said. "If Sherlock is still inside, he will find his way out sooner or later."

"Or maybe he will get arrested," Lupin muttered nervously.

We talked about this and that, hoping that our friend would find his way out of the Royal Opera House, but soon it was time for lunch, and I had to return to the hotel.

"Can I ask you a question, Lupin?" I said before saying goodbye.

"Of course."

"The writer who allowed us to go inside — Collins. Did you really know him?"

My friend laughed, and pulled from his pocket a small book with a dark cover. *The Moonstone,* signed by Wilkie Collins.

"I took it from his jacket pocket," he said. "And

when I heard his name, I tried it. A writer who brings a copy of his own book with him is a writer who dreams of being flattered, I told myself. And so it was!"

I watched Lupin, full of admiration, and I wondered if my friends would ever cease to amaze me with their fearlessness and intelligence.

Then, before heading to the hotel, I lingered in front of the magnificent theater, wondering where Sherlock Holmes might be hiding inside.

## Chapter 19

# DARKNESS BEHIND THE CURTAIN

The process of waiting, that afternoon confirmed for me, slows time down to an unbearable rate. The seconds become minutes, minutes become hours, and so on.

I knew Sherlock. If he remained in that theater, it was because he had a plan up his sleeve. And I could not wait to find out what that plan was. As I walked back to the hotel, I went over the possibilities in my mind.

When I got to the Claridge's, I read and reread the telegram from my father a thousand times. He wrote that he and Mother were stranded in Calais because of the rough seas and that they would be off to London as soon as the weather improved over the English Channel. Then I tried to entertain myself by paging through my guide to London and chatting with Mr. Nelson, but the sleepy atmosphere of the hotel soon made me antsy.

I said goodbye to Mr. Nelson, and for once I told him the truth — I was going out for a walk. But at the end of this walk, I found myself standing in front of the Shackleton Coffee House. When I walked into the café, there was no sign of Sherlock or Lupin. And so I had to wait again, but this time in the company of a cup of hot cocoa. Thankfully, I didn't have to wait long, and when I saw my friends enter the café, I noticed something in their eyes immediately — there was some interesting news.

My two friends joined me, and Sherlock placed an old bronze key on the table next to my now-empty mug.

"Since you're in London to sightsee, how about a visit to the Royal Opera House?" he asked.

"What a question!" I said excitedly. "Let's go there now!"

But I soon learned that it was not possible to go there immediately. While Sherlock had been hiding in the theater, in addition to stealing a key to the back door, he had heard bits of conversation between some musicians. At five o'clock the orchestra would be done rehearsing, and the theater would then be empty. So we waited until five o'clock, drinking hot cocoa and getting lost in all kinds of theories relating to our investigation.

When it was finally five o'clock, we left the café and reached Covent Garden by carriage. When we arrived, the last of the musicians were saying their goodbyes in front of the theater. Once they were gone, we moved fast among the first coils of fog that were beginning to surround the city.

Lupin and I kept watch while Sherlock opened the door.

A few moments later, the three of us were inside, surrounded by almost complete darkness.

"Come on! I think I know where the wardrobe is," Sherlock told us softly. "This way!"

We followed and found ourselves surrounded by the eerie, partly dismantled scenes of the stage. Some pieces of the set were attached to ropes that disappeared into the darkness above us. It felt like we were walking in a cemetery made of painted canvasses and wooden shapes. With each step, the stage floor creaked slightly with an unsettling sound.

Sherlock brought us to a steep and narrow metal ladder that led underground. He climbed down first, hunching his shoulders to avoid hitting his head against the low-vaulted ceiling.

The basement hallway was cluttered with stage tools, mirrors, mannequins, and drapes, and because of the darkness, it was difficult to walk. The soft lights at the ends of the corridor were barely enough to see by.

We reached a point where the corridor forked. Straight ahead led to the dressing rooms while turning right led to a lower basement. Sherlock pointed to the right, and I swallowed hard, trying to keep my breath quiet as it became more labored and heavy. We had just started on the new staircase when we heard some voices.

"Shh!" Sherlock hissed, making a sign with his hand to stop.

We tried to figure out where they were coming from, but the way sounds echoed between those narrow corridors made it difficult to know with any certainty.

Soon we were back at the fork in the corridor, crouching in the shadows. We heard two voices — one male and one female — coming from the stairs.

"Is that Collins?" I asked, whispering into Sherlock's ear.

"I can't say," Sherlock replied. "He has an accent."

"Italian," Lupin said, sure of himself.

He was right.

A few moments later we heard the woman's voice say the word "maestro." I looked at my friends. The man who was coming up the stairs from the basement was Giuseppe Barzini. I leaned over to look down the hallway and saw the luminous glow of an oil lamp crawling slowly up the stairs.

Sherlock turned rapidly and looked down the corridor behind us, his eyes glittering in the dark. "Did you hear something?" he asked.

But neither Lupin nor I could take our eyes off of the two figures on the staircase.

"How can you deny it, my dear?" Maestro Barzini said. "It is useless to deny that we are all very worried. I was wondering if you, being such a dear friend to

Ophelia, know something more than what Scotland Yard has told us."

"No, Maestro. As I said, I know nothing more. Nor how she is doing or where they have brought her," the woman replied.

The Maestro sighed. "All this is terrible," he said. "Terrible and painful."

The oil lamp swung.

"I have worked with Ophelia for almost twenty years, and I find it humiliating that the police treat me like I'm the last of the curious. Forced to beg for scraps of news about my poor student like an ordinary stranger! Does that seem right, my dear?" Barzini said.

"No, Maestro," the woman agreed. "It does not. On the contrary, I say that after what has happened, Scotland Yard should also protect you!"

"You are kind, my dear . . . but that does not really matter," replied the musician. "To see Ophelia, to know that she's all right . . . that's all I want right now," he concluded with another sigh.

If they had taken just a few more steps, they would have reached us at the fork in the corridor. Sherlock, Lupin, and I silently consulted about where to hide next. We stepped back a few feet in the dark, hoping that the two would go in the direction of the dressing rooms.

"You will see that everything will be all for the best, Maestro," the lady said with a polite tone.

"I would like to believe you, my dear!" he replied.

"You have to be strong in moments like these, Maestro."

They stopped just before the fork.

"You promise that if you ever hear about Ophelia, you will tell me?" asked Maestro Barzini, his voice sorrowful.

"You will be the first to know," the woman assured him, walking with him to the doors of the dressing rooms.

I breathed a sigh of relief.

Prodding me to follow him, Sherlock tugged at the hem of my skirt. We crawled on all fours to the hallway that led to the basement, and we hid there, remaining motionless in the dark. We listened carefully, but from that position we could only hear a faint hum.

After a while, we heard some steps, then the voice of the woman again, now very close by. "Goodbye,

Maestro and, I pray, do not worry yourself too much," she said, taking her leave. Then we heard her walking along the corridor in the opposite direction.

"Shall we go down?" Lupin asked once the steps of the woman sounded far away.

"In the dark?" I asked.

"It's only dark until the end of the staircase," Sherlock explained. We agreed to wait a few minutes before making a move so we wouldn't run into Barzini coming out of the dressing room.

Suddenly, there was a loud noise. The crash of glass breaking. All three of us jumped. The shattering was followed by a scream. Immediately, I thought about what the woman had just said to Barzini, "Scotland Yard should also protect you."

"No! Not him now!" I said, with a strangled cry.

Sherlock and Lupin looked at each other.

"Did you hear that rumbling noise?" Sherlock asked.

"No. But perhaps the attacker is hidden, lurking," Lupin said.

That word, "attacker," nearly made my heart stop. I closed my eyes and saw the Spaniard. I could picture him hidden in the shadows of the haunting stage sets. He might have gone down to Barzini's dressing room to kill him, too, after murdering his assistant and making an attempt to kill Ophelia Merridew. That thought made me freeze, petrified with terror.

Lupin suddenly made a move toward the dressing rooms.

"Freeze! Wait!" Sherlock whispered, grabbing him by the arm.

Lupin had just enough time to crouch down into darkness again when the door to Barzini's dressing room opened.

We stood motionless in the dark while Barzini staggered into the corridor and passed by our hiding place, cursing softly. We watched him disappear in the direction of the stage. I noticed that one of his hands was bandaged with a rag. Red with blood.

"Let's help him!" I said, fearing I might lose consciousness at any moment. "And get out of here!"

"Quiet, Irene," Lupin said, shaking me. "There seems to be no one else . . ."

"True," Sherlock agreed. "It's quiet down here."

Sherlock and Lupin went together and peered around the corner. Then they moved quickly toward the dressing room, dragging me with them. I was totally opposed to that decision, but I did not have the energy to resist.

All I could do was go along with them. My heart beat so violently, I thought it might break out of my chest and onto the floor.

"And now what?" I whispered.

We reached the door of Barzini's dressing room. There were a few drops of blood on the floor. Lupin pulled a pair of white gloves from his pocket, put them on, and gently pushed the door open.

"I do not think this is a good idea," I whispered, afraid of being attacked at any moment by the mysterious criminal who was hunting the artists of the Royal Opera House.

Instead I saw only Barzini's dressing room, lit by the oil lamp that he had been holding just a few minutes before. The room was empty.

"Look!" Lupin exclaimed. He pointed to a broken mirror next to a music stand.

Sherlock picked up a bloody splinter of glass from the ground and muttered, "He injured himself."

Just then, in a corner of the room that until that moment had been hidden from my view by the silhouette of Sherlock Holmes, I saw some familiar clothes tossed in a heap atop an old wooden chair.

It took a few moments, but when I finally began to process what my eyes were seeing, I could not help myself and I screamed.

# Chapter 20

# THE DEVIL'S COSTUME

Thrown on top of the chair were a long black cloak, a red scarf, and a hat with a wide brim. Sherlock, Lupin, and I looked at each other, stunned.

"But — but then . . ." I stammered.

"The Spaniard is him! It's Barzini!" Sherlock exclaimed.

"Curse him!" Lupin mumbled between his teeth, his face flushing. "CURSE HIM!" he shouted. He sprinted out of the room like an angry beast. Neither Sherlock nor I managed to restrain him in time. He ran down the corridor that led to the stage. We could not do anything but follow our friend and his distressed cries that echoed through the corridors like those of a wounded animal.

When we caught up with him, Lupin had just spotted Barzini behind the scenes of the stage, and was staring at him from afar with eyes full of anger.

The Maestro stood at a porcelain basin with his back to us, washing his bloody fingers.

Lupin stepped forward.

Hearing his steps, the Maestro whipped his head around, surprised. "Who the hell are you?"

"Does the name Théophraste Lupin mean anything to you?" Lupin roared.

Barzini turned completely and wrapped his hand in a handkerchief. "Should it?" he asked.

"He is the man that got put in prison instead of you! Charged with *your* murder of Santi!"

"I do not know what you're talking about, young man. And above all . . . what are you still doing in the theater at this hour? The workers should all be out already!"

"What workers?! I am the son of Théophraste Lupin! And I have exposed you!" Lupin shouted.

Barzini laughed, wiping his hands. "You have

exposed me? I insist — I do not understand what you mean!"

"You are the Spaniard who framed my father!" Lupin shouted.

"I am sorry to disappoint you, but I'll have you know that I am Italian," Barzini muttered scornfully. "And now, if you do not mind — get out of here, before I am forced to call the Scotland Yard."

"Actually, that is exactly what we would like to do!" exclaimed Sherlock Holmes, who was alongside Lupin at that point.

I saw Giuseppe Barzini hesitate and take a step back. "May I know what's going on?" he muttered when I approached my friends. The theater was dimly lit, but it is likely that as he looked at us, Barzini began to suspect that we were the same people who he had surprised in Bethnal Green.

"It so happens that we figured out your plan, Maestro Barzini," Sherlock Holmes said calmly. "We know that you hired Théophraste Lupin to carry out a theft, but that it was actually a trap to blame him for something far worse — for the murder of Alfred Santi. We know that you tried to kill Ophelia Merridew, and now you want to know where she is hiding — to shut her up when she recovers!"

"Enough of this nonsense!" the Maestro snapped. "You are only three stupid children with your heads full of fantasies!"

"Three stupid children who have exposed your crimes!" I said.

"Anyway, your charade is over, Maestro!" Sherlock yelled. "The evening papers have just reported the news . . . Ophelia has woken up. And when she can talk, she will reveal you as the killer — as you well know!"

Those words seemed to hit Barzini like a stab in the chest. The musician's eyes widened. He looked lost and, groping behind him, leaned against the basin. His reaction in that moment revealed his guilt more than any confession in words could.

The musician put a hand in the pocket of his waistcoat and pulled out a gold watch. After consulting it with a feverish look, he burst out laughing — a crazy laugh that echoed in the wings of the theater, making my skin crawl.

"You are smart, boy," Barzini said to Sherlock. "But the news you are talking about was not in the newspapers as of four o'clock, and now it's five-thirty. The second edition will be released in only half an hour," he concluded, revealing Sherlock's bluff.

But the musician already knew we had exposed his guilt. Still laughing in that horrible manner, Barzini turned abruptly, and with surprising agility for his age, he disappeared between the pieces of scenery.

We heard his voice resound through the theater: "You really think you can bring down the great Barzini? How much arrogance you young people have! Arrogance! Just like Santi, that ungrateful fool! Instead of being honored to work beside me . . . pah!"

Lupin ran between the objects and the shadows of the stage, trying to spot Barzini so he could try to catch him. Sherlock and I did the same, staying a few steps behind our friend.

Meanwhile, furious noises began to echo in the theater, as if Barzini was knocking down any object that happened to come within his range.

Actually, he was looking for something. We figured that out, when, after a few moments of silence, the musician reappeared in front of Sherlock, holding a sword in his good hand.

Sherlock, caught off guard, took a step back and tripped on a rope, tumbling onto the stage.

I saw Barzini raise the weapon, ready to strike.

"NO!" I cried. And without even knowing what I was doing, I grabbed the object nearest to me — a chair — and threw it at him with all my strength.

I missed by a small margin, but I still forced him to dodge it, and that gave Sherlock time to stand and pick up a wooden board.

"Back! Stand back, Irene!" Sherlock yelled at me.

Barzini plunged forward with the sword, but Sherlock was able to deflect and then attack with some lunges. Sherlock moved nimbly, dodging Barzini's blows as he weaved in and out of the scenery.

I stood watching my friend defend himself, and with every assault from Barzini, I felt my heart beating furiously. I was wondering, exasperated, where on Earth Lupin was, when I found myself face to face with a little man who looked at me with tiny, pleading eyes.

"Duvel?" I asked. "What are you doing here?"

His eyes seemed possessed, and his face ashen. He looked like he was about to faint. "I've heard everything . . ." he whispered.

"So help us, Duvel!" I said, irritated by his cowardice. "Go call Scotland Yard — and hurry!"

"Come with me, young lady! Please!" he begged.

"Run and call Scotland Yard! Now!" I hissed.

Then I pushed him away and went back to watch what was happening with Sherlock and Barzini. In between deflecting one blow after another from Barzini's sword, Sherlock kept throwing quick glances toward the ceiling. Looking up to see why, I spotted Lupin perched on a beam above the stage — he was guiding Sherlock's movements.

Barzini was now plunging his strikes with more fury. "You're finished!" he cried when he managed to hit Sherlock in the shoulder, tearing his jacket and shirt and scratching his skin, which spurted a little gush of blood.

Sherlock felt the wound, lowering the weapon and backing away as fast as he could. In a matter of seconds, Barzini was lunging at Sherlock trying to land a decisive blow. My friend slipped out of the way just in time and rolled behind a large column.

The musician screamed. "Where are you going? Now I come to get —"

But he could not finish the sentence. Lupin,

SHERLOCK, LUPIN & ME

clinging to a rope, hovered over Barzini, surprising him from behind. Barzini fell onto the floor in fright, releasing his grip on the sword, which flew a few feet in front of him. I ran over, grabbed the weapon, and threw it into the orchestra pit.

Lupin then pounced on Barzini, pushed him onto his back, pinned him down on the ground, and tied his scarf around his wrists. At that point, Sherlock emerged from behind the column holding a heavy cloth torn from a piece of the set. He gave it to Lupin who used it to bind Barzini's legs, while the Maestro shouted words in Italian that did not sound at all polite.

"Good timing, Lupin . . ." I muttered.

Sherlock Holmes ran to grab the rope that had tripped him and handed it to Lupin, who used it to tie Barzini's ankles together, who was squirming like he was being bit by a tarantula.

"So. Now what?" Sherlock asked then, the calmness in his voice displaying his usual hint of irony.

"Someone will have to go and call Scotland Yard," Lupin muttered.

"Duvel!" I replied. "He went there."

My friends looked at me, astonished. "Duvel? And where does Duvel fit in?"

I had no time to explain it. We heard noises coming from outside and from behind the stage. We turned in circles looking for the source of the noise, but nobody was there.

Then we heard a distant door open, and an inspector from the Scotland Yard yelled into the theater. "Hold it!"

"Apparently they are already here!" I exclaimed.

All three of us looked at the strange, kicking bundle that Barzini had become. He would not be going anywhere except straight into the arms of the police.

The three of us, on the other hand, could move just fine. And we did not lose a moment to do so.

We ran at breathless speed toward the back door, praying that the police had not already surrounded the entire building. Sherlock pushed the door open with his shoulder, and the three of us found ourselves outside in the dense mist that now surrounded the city.

# Chapter 21

# LIKE A DREAM

The morning after those events occurred, a couple of local newspapers had been tipped off and had come out with a special edition.

"Have you read this, Miss Irene?" Mr. Nelson asked me at breakfast. The paper was still hot from the press, and the large, dark letters of the headlines left spots on my fingertips.

"Ophelia Merridew regained consciousness," continued Mr. Nelson. "They are expecting 'shocking revelations from the singer'!"

"Yes," I muttered in resposne. "It seems that

nothing happens in this city without the journalists knowing about it."

"Modern times, Miss Irene, modern times . . ." Mr. Nelson said, followed by a brief sigh.

"They also have their positives, these modern times," I replied.

"What do you mean, Miss?"

"The newspaper also reports the address of the place where Merridew has been hiding and the exact time it is expected she will leave to go home," I said.

"So . . ."

"So this will be an important event for London. And for us, as future Londoners! I do not think we should miss it, my dear Horatio!"

He looked at me, puzzled, then smiled. He must have thought that waiting in front of a house was, after all, better than taking me shopping!

"I'll call a carriage, Miss," he said.

Even though I was supposed to meet Sherlock and Lupin at Shackleton's that day, I thought it likely that they, too, had heard the news about Ophelia.

Mr. Nelson and I got ready quickly, hopped into the carriage, and headed toward Whitechapel — the location of Ophelia Merridew. When we arrived, there was already a large crowd of curious people. Merridew's refuge was a three-story building with white windows and a blue door, which indicated that it was owned by the queen.

Every time a shadow passed behind the lace curtains, a timid applause emerged from the crowd, and someone shouted, "Ophelia!" hoping to see, sooner or later, the singer finally free from danger.

I looked around the crowd. They were all ordinary people — people who had probably never seen Ophelia perform. But these people knew that Ophelia was one of them, and they knew that she never had forgotten her roots.

This was, pretty much, what Mr. Nelson said to me, while we were waiting for something to happen. He insisted that a person's true roots are links that, though they may be invisible, never cease to operate between a person and his or her origins.

It was mid-morning when Ophelia Merridew appeared at the door, escorted by a nurse who helped steady her. She looked pale and in pain, but smiled a little and made a small gesture of greeting. The crowd responded with applause, full of emotion.

I looked at Mr. Nelson, as if to ask permission to

get closer, and he said kindly, "Go, go! You came all this way for her, after all!"

And so I got off the carriage, squeezing through the crowd. I do not know what came over me then. All I know is that I felt an impulse to get as close to Ophelia as I could. It took determination and some good elbow strikes, but I finally managed to get to the front, where a police barricade barely held back the crowd. I felt very excited to see Miss Merridew safe and sound again after our last tragic encounter.

"Ophelia!" I called, imitating those around me. While the singer was slowly heading to her carriage, something happened that I still remember with great emotion.

She turned toward me. Toward *me*, I tell you. And when she saw me, her eyes looked full of surprise, and her gaze remained on my face.

Ophelia Merridew recognized me among all those people. And so, if only for a moment, I was a little bit famous.

She approached me, accompanied by the nurse, and gave me her hand. "Are you . . . I still see your face . . . like that of an angel," Ophelia said. "An angel who came to save me in Bethnal Green."

"My name is Irene," I said. I smiled at her.

Ophelia showed me to the blue door from which she had come out. "Would you like to come in? We need to talk. My carriage can wait!" she insisted.

I ducked under the outstretched arms of a police officer and joined Ophelia, who took me by the arm, welcoming me. We went through the blue door and sat in a small living room.

Ophelia said goodbye to the nurse and, once we were left alone, she looked at me tenderly. "Tell me everything, my young angel."

I described all that had happened until that fateful afternoon, when we had arrived just in time at her Aunt Betty's home. Then I told her about all that had happened since, including the plot of the Maestro.

"My friends and I heard Barzini say that poor Alfred Santi was a magnificent man and he was punished for it, but . . . what that might mean, we do not know," I said.

Ophelia Merridew looked down before speaking. "There are many things you do not know, and you would never have known them, my young angel," she said. "There was a secret . . . a secret that Barzini did not want revealed to anyone . . ."

I expected that she would confess to meeting secretly with Santi, and that what was born between them had sparked the jealousy of Maestro Barzini. But I was surprised when Ophelia, with a simple sentence, revealed that this secret hid a different story, and with it, the real motive behind the evil that took place.

"Barzini's latest works were not, in fact, written by him. And that is why they are probably among the most beautiful he has ever had his name on," Ophelia explained.

I suddenly remembered what Baron Trudoljubov had said about the "second youth" of Barzini, and my eyes widened in surprise.

"The most recent two works that everybody thought were composed by Barzini were, in fact, composed by my poor Alfred," she told me, her voice cracking.

I took her hand and looked into her eyes. "If you find it too painful, you do not have to . . ." I said as I shook my head.

"On the contrary," Ophelia said, wiping away her tears. "On the contrary . . . I feel it will do me good to talk to you, Irene."

I squeezed her hand more tightly, and she began to speak.

"At the beginning, Alfred had been honored to work side by side with the famous Barzini — the great Maestro! Who would not have been? But as time passed, it became clear that Barzini was using him. Barzini's inspiration had dried up, and he began to take credit for Alfred's works. Alfred realized that his talent would never be recognized like that — like Barzini's had been. Month after month, Barzini promised to print Santi's name next to his, indicating the two of them as composers. But he never kept his promise. Santi became more and more determined to get recognition as time went on. And then that snake Barzini hired the petty Henri Duvel. He did so only to make Alfred believe that his position was in danger. And so Alfred worked. But finally he realized Barzini still needed him, and he mustered the strength to rebel against him. Alfred refused to give him his last composition, a work called *Semiramide*."

*That's why Santi was always so dark and angry*, I thought while listening to the story. *He was at odds with Barzini!*

"The Maestro then lied to Alfred one last time,"

Ophelia continued. "Barzini had assured Alfred that this time, his name would be featured on posters at the largest theaters in Europe. Alfred was convinced that Barzini was serious." Ophelia smiled bitterly before continuing, "But Barzini had no intention of keeping his promise even at that time. He confessed it to me one night at dinner after having one drink too many. He said Alfred had learned everything he knew about music from him, and that he was ungrateful for it. He regarded Alfred in the usual dismissive way he treated all those who worked for him. He treated them all as his subjects — as if he were the sole, undisputed King of the Opera!"

Ophelia drew a long breath in and then exhaled. "It was Barzini's own fault. Because he was so blinded by his own ego, his own fame, he hadn't even realized that Alfred and I had become much more than friends over time. Alfred loved me and I . . . well, I loved him with a strength that I thought my aging heart was no longer capable of. I loved him, Irene. And that's why I warned him about Barzini's true intentions. I told him not to give Barzini his last work, to hold on to it, and, if necessary, to hide the score in a safe place."

"And did he do it?" I asked, captivated. "Did Santi really hide his last work before . . . before . . ."

Ophelia nodded slowly.

"Yes. He hid it by giving it to me. And I . . . when Alfred was found dead in his hotel room and the Frenchman was arrested, I thought I might go crazy. Everything seemed so absurd and terrible. I just wanted to hide, disappear, and not imagine that Barzini would . . ." She paused, then continued. "Luckily, I handed Alfred's work off to a trusted person who has kept it safe so far," Ophelia explained.

"That's why Santi's hotel room and your aunt's house in Bethnal Green had been turned upside down!" I exclaimed. "Barzini was looking for Alfred Santi's latest work!"

"That's right, Irene."

I looked at her, waiting.

And then, because it seemed that Ophelia Merridew did not have anything more to say, I asked her, without hesitation, "And where did you hide the score in the end?"

# Chapter 22

# ONE LAST CUP OF COCOA

Lupin barged into the Shackleton Coffee House so quickly he almost spilled Sherlock's beloved cup of hot cocoa upon arriving at our table.

"My father is all right!" he yelled. He hurriedly pulled a chair up to the table Sherlock and I were sitting at. "My father is all right!"

We all hugged one another, and then sat down, listening carefully to the details of Lupin's story. With the capture of Barzini, the murder charges against Théophraste were soon dropped.

"The 'attempted theft' charge remains," admitted

Lupin. "But for that, he would spend just a few days in jail and —"

Lupin seemed to want to say more, but when he realized that other customers were listening to him as well, he went silent, visibly embarrassed.

"How about we go for a walk?" Sherlock suggested, throwing a few coins on the table.

As we walked through the shady avenues of Hyde Park, we cleared up the final obscure details of that story.

"If Barzini did not know about the relationship between Santi and Ophelia, as she told me," I reasoned, "he would not have to fear her. And he wouldn't have suspected that she might have the scores of *Semiramide*."

Sherlock, of course, had thought of that detail, and shared his reasoning with us.

"When he orchestrated the plot at Hotel Albion," he explained, "Barzini searched Santi's room, but he did not find the new work. Instead what he found were notes and letters to Santi in Miss Merridew's handwriting."

"Of course!" I nodded. "Letters between the two lovers."

"Exactly," Sherlock agreed. "And so he discovered that he had a new enemy . . . one who he needed to get rid of quickly."

He paused, thinking. "Poor Ophelia must have been terribly confused in those hours," Sherlock continued. "She had warned Santi about Barzini, as Irene said, which indicates she was suspicious of him. On the other hand, Scotland Yard already had its guilty man, a French acrobat who had nothing to do with Barzini. And that's what pulled the wool over Merridew's eyes."

We went farther into the park, leaving behind us, little by little, the noise of the city. We came to a meadow by the shelter of an old oak tree and sat there on the ground, continuing to mull over what had happened.

"Yes, I'm convinced," I finally said. "Ophelia's instinct must have led her to believe it was a good idea to hide *Semiramide,* so that Barzini would not take possession of the last opera composed by her beloved Alfred. Unfortunately, she did not realize how dangerous this man was . . ."

"And when Ophelia felt in danger," Sherlock added, "her aunt's empty house must've seemed like the perfect hiding place for her and for Santi's work. After all, who would guess that Ophelia Merridew would be holed up in a hovel in Bethnal Green?"

"Yes. But unfortunately for her, she already had a thorn in her side — the devil!" said Lupin. "But," he continued, scratching his head, "there's another thing I just don't understand . . . why did my father think that Barzini was a Spaniard?"

Sherlock gave us one of his enigmatic smiles. I could not imagine how my friend might have an answer to that question also. But just a moment later, the answer came from a pocket in his jacket, like a rabbit out of a hat. It was a copy of the *British Musical Gazette,* a magazine that had published a biography of Barzini.

"Giuseppe Barzini lived with his parents in Seville from when he was nine to sixteen years old," Sherlock said, "and he was therefore able to speak excellent Spanish. I think he used this skill to confuse your father, Lupin. And I would say that he did it perfectly."

The most important question, however, was the one I had asked Merridew just a few hours earlier.

"What do you think happened to the score of the

latest work by Alfred Santi?" I asked them, fiddling with some blades of grass.

"What did Merridew say?" Lupin asked.

"I've already told you — she handed it over to a person she trusts blindly, and she will never reveal its location." I looked at my friends hopelessly. "Not even to right the wrongs done or to make sure Santi would at least have the fame to which he's entitled."

"But why?" Lupin asked.

"Ophelia considers it a cursed manuscript and says that no one, after what has happened, would ever have the courage to take it to the stage," I replied.

"The usual superstitions die hard," Sherlock muttered, annoyed, "especially in the world of entertainment."

"Then we give up?" Lupin asked.

Sherlock opened his arms in response, shrugging.

They both looked at me. "What do you say?"

"I say that we may have more to think about right now. Your father is finally safe, and mine comes to town in just a few hours," I said. I had almost forgotten that London would become, at least for a while, my new city.

We said goodbye, planning to meet at the usual place the following day. Sherlock walked with me for a stretch, but then visited a library where he wanted to consult some book. I was beginning to get my bearings on those streets, and I had almost arrived at my hotel when I came across Lupin.

It was not an accidental encounter. Lupin was waiting for me, and he was visibly uncomfortable. I was uncomfortable, too, but more because of the great anxiety that I could read on his face.

We walked toward each other and then stopped. He looked up at the sky and then at his shoes. He put his hands on his head and then hugged his shoulders. He did practically everything he could so he wouldn't have to look at me while he spoke.

"I understand if you do not want to have anything to do with me, the son of a thief," he finally said.

I looked at him with my mouth wide open, shocked, searching for the words to tell him how terribly wrong he was.

I decided to settle on the first words that came to my lips — the most sincere words. "Tell me now, Arsène Lupin, are you, perhaps, senile?" I asked, putting my fists on my hips. "You could very well be the son of the fierce Saladin, and I would not give a hoot, nor would I let it change our friendship."

Lupin gave me one of his charming smiles and said simply, "Thank you, Irene. Tomorrow I go on the road. I hope we meet again soon."

As I finished my walk back to the hotel, I began to think that if only I had been a bit more careful during my first adventure in London, I could have understood many more things about my family, my friends, and myself.

★ ★ ★

My parents joined Mr. Nelson and me at the Claridge's that night. The next day, at first light, we visited what would become our new apartment. It was completely empty, but it had a spectacular view over the rooftops of the city and of the distant clock, Big Ben. When I saw it I shouted, "Yes! I love it!"

Mr. Nelson had done an excellent job. The room that would become my room was just above the courtyard, which made me hopeful that my secret exits might be a bit easier than usual to carry out.

It is not about this new home I want to write, however. What I choose to write about to conclude this story still makes my heart beat fast, even years and years later.

It was the day the postman delivered a mysterious package addressed to me at that new apartment in London. In one corner of the package was the sender's name: "The Prince of Riddles."

When I opened it, I thought it might be one of Sherlock Holmes's usual tricks, but instead, I found that the package held a manuscript entitled *Semiramide,* by Alfred Santi, and a handwritten note by my fellow investigator, who, apparently, had not abandoned the search for the last missing piece of the mystery.

*If you want to know where and how I found it, meet tomorrow at noon at the Shackleton Coffee House.*

This just made me more curious, and the wait even more difficult. In fact, I spent a sleepless night wondering how he had managed to find the manuscript and to whom Ophelia Merridew had entrusted it. At last, as we sat at a table in the Shackleton Coffee House the next day, Sherlock Holmes finally revealed the secret.

"You remember the famous Aunt Betty?" he said, smiling. He reached out and almost brushed my fingers, he was so excited. "The one we thought was at the hospital? Well, she was not. While she had always been a bit strange and eccentric, a few years ago, after an earthquake, she developed claustrophobia — a fear of staying indoors. So she began to live on the streets as a beggar. But even though she preferred to stay outside, she was never far away from her home. You could say that she simply moved back and forth on the sidewalk in front of her house."

My eyes widened. "You mean . . . the beggar in Bethnal Green? She had Santi's work?"

Sherlock laced his fingers behind his head, satisfied. "The beggar on the street corner," he said.

I smiled, breathing in the rich vapor released by my steaming cup of cocoa. I began to think of Lupin, back on the road with his father and the Aronofsky Circus. Were the three of us going to see each other again? Or would this be the end of our crazy adventures together?

All these questions would be answered soon enough, as the thread of my destiny unfolded bit by bit.

IRENE ADLER

# SHERLOCK, LUPIN & ME

## KEEP YOUR EYES PEELED FOR THE NEXT BOOK IN THE SHERLOCK, LUPIN & ME SERIES!

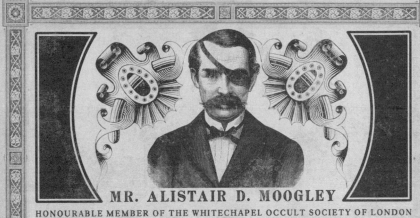